Dear Rhian
All the best
Love
Hannah
x x x

YOUR WORST FEARS

HANNAH COSTIN

VELOX BOOKS
Published by arrangement with the author.

Your Worst Fears copyright © 2021
by Hannah Costin.

All Rights Reserved.

This book is a work of fiction. People, places, events, and situations are the product of the author's imagination. Any resemblance to actual persons, living or dead, or historical events, is purely coincidental.

No part of this book may be reproduced, stored in a retrieval system, or transmitted by any means without the written permission of the author and publisher.

CONTENTS

I'm a Fucking Machine 1
Everyday Charlotte's Mother Forgot to Collect Her from School . 6
Are You Sitting Comfortably? 11
My Worst Fear 17
Snapchat Filters 22
Blended Families 27
My Friend the Scarecrow 37
The Man in the Shed 43
Angeli 52
The Regulars 56
I Hate Being Picked Last 63
I'm One of Four Sisters and We Were All Born Cursed 68
Please Don't Let This Fail 80
She Always Held a Hammer 86
My Sister Lottie 90
The Homeless Woman 93
My Boy Teddy 97
A Late-Night Dog Walk 102
Letters to Annabelle 108

Don't Forget to Feed the Fish	114
The Hotel Neighbour	119
The Black Cat	126
New Year's Eve, 2020	131
Insane in the Mundane	136
The Littlest Sheet Ghost	140
There's a Nefarious Chicken on my Lawn	147
The Story of April Strange	151
Run	159
My Last Passenger was a Nightmare	164
The Portal	173

I'M A FUCKING MACHINE

Short skirt. Thigh high suspenders. Killer heels. Long, thick black hair. She had pulled out all the stops. The type of girl that made even a stone-cold bastard like me consider revising my one-night policy.

The fucking was formulaic. Work them up, get them moaning, erupt, get them out, rinse and repeat. I recognise that most people think men like me are disgusting. But I bet more are jealous of my consistent success than they would care to admit.

I wish I felt as disgusted by my behaviour as others did. I wish I felt at all. Had I become so detached that the only thing that made me feel alive was my dick? It certainly consumed my thoughts. Was my lack of concern a reason to worry?

I tried to work out where it all went wrong. To ponder which event in my life had turned me into this soulless fuck machine, but I kept coming up blank. Instead, was nothing but a dreamy montage of gorgeous one-night stands.

I didn't know why I was like this. Why I was in the same spot in the same bar the very next night? Why hadn't the girl in the suspenders been enough? I struggled to fathom my insatiable desire and pondered a cause, getting nowhere. Maybe the answer was in the blonde girl's panties.

She was cute. More enthusiastic than most, and I liked that. She beamed during the taxi ride home and danced into my apartment. She was so full of vibrant personality that I wished I had.

Peeling off her clothes felt good. She kept intense eye contact throughout. She was so damn hot I felt about ready to explode.

Afterwards, she wanted to cuddle. So many of them do.

She nuzzled her head into my arm and ran the fingers of her other hand along my bare chest. It was sensual. I almost felt ready for a second round. But my code of conduct was strict. It couldn't be rewritten.

She had served her purpose. Terrible as it sounded, I was onto my next incredibly important mission. Get rid of her. It was always a compulsion that struck quickly post coitus.

"It's time to go baby, I'll call you a cab."

I got up. Picked up my boxers off the floor and dressed. The routine was infallible.

Until it wasn't.

Her eyes glazed, she pulled the duvet up to her chin and looked downwards. She started to cry.

It was a scenario I hadn't expected. I was used to being called an arsehole... amongst other, less pleasant names. But not tears. Most of them didn't want to show weakness like that. Heck, most of them wanted the same *fucking* thing I did.

She didn't though. She wanted more. I don't know how she expected to find what she was looking for sitting alone in dive bars, but I knew I had seriously misjudged her intentions.

Blondie was different. I wish I had gotten her name, but that had never been a piece of information that I chose to retain. I asked, of course, but never absorbed.

"Don't you like me?" She sobbed, mascara running down her pretty face.

"Of course I do. But you know what this is, right?"

I didn't look her in the eyes. I should've known better; someone as *smooth* as I liked to think I was should've been able to charm himself out of the situation. I just couldn't find the words. It was something that happened to me so many times before. I found that after I'd picked girls up, I just didn't know what to do with them.

That sounds bad. They're humans. Real people. It's a reflection on me more than anything. On the lack of depth that led to my next actions.

I left her alone in that room to dress herself. Not a single other word. Humiliated. Crying. I should've known what all those behaviours meant. But I was emotionally devoid.

I walked to the kitchen and set out two glasses of water. One for her when she emerged, to wash down the alcohol before she embarked on the cab ride of shame. I thought I was doing a damn good thing. Considerate.

"You're a piece of shit."

The voice came from behind me. I turned to face her. Her eyes were wide and glazed with tears. Her expression manic.

She took me by surprise when she plunged the knife into my chest. I felt the blade pierce my skin, but I didn't feel the pain that I expected would come with it. Where did she get the knife? It wasn't one of mine. Who brings a knife to a bar?

I tried to process but nothing would compute. It didn't make sense. Was I being hunted? Was the type of girl that I hunted for hunting for a guy like me herself?

Blondie's attack came as a nasty surprise.

Not nearly as much surprise, however, as I felt when literal sparks flew. Still not a glimmer of pain. Why didn't it hurt? Were they... wires?

She looked surprised too. I don't think they were the type of sparks that blondie had been anticipating from a romantic evening. Her eyes went from frenzied to frightened in seconds. There was a flurry of sound and movement.

Men entered. They wore white hazmat suits and masks. I don't know how the fuck they got in my flat or how they appeared so quickly with no noise. The only thing that made sense was if they'd been inside the entire time and that's a thought that continues to fuck with me.

One grabbed blondie and dragged her away and the other stuck a needle in my neck. Everything went black. My muscles seized up and I hit the ground. I suspect the intention was to render me unconscious, but I was merely paralysed.

"I thought you said it could weed out the crazy ones. We don't want that in the gene pool! Now she has to be disposed of. You put this whole operation at risk, you idiot!"

I couldn't open my eyes to see who the voice was coming from or move my mouth to ask questions. I was incapable of making a sound. I just knew that the first voice came from whoever had injected me.

And a different voice answered.

"Don't speak to me like that. Without me you wouldn't even have an operation. We couldn't have predicted this. It needs an update. Wipe it, reset it, we'll have it back out in the field by tomorrow."

I could feel the dragging. But I still couldn't move. Still couldn't feel any pain. In fact, when I put some thought into it, I wasn't sure I'd ever felt actual pain.

Why were there wires inside of me?

I felt every prod, poke, incision. Wherever they took me, I stayed for a while. It may have been hours or even days. The concept of time was immeasurable in my prison of a body.

I felt it all. Everything. Everything but the pain. I didn't hear those two voices again. I don't know at what point I went to sleep, but eventually there were no more memories. No more awareness.

When I woke up in my apartment it was as if nothing had happened. It was like a surreal dream. No blood from blondie's attack… no blondie. I wonder what happened to her. No scar on my chest. No knife. Nothing.

Had I imagined it? Did I fail to score at the bar and drown my sorrows? I wasn't sure it was physically possible to consume the alcohol required for a vision so strong.

I would've probably dismissed the whole bizarre event had it not been for blondie's pink lace thong that had been kicked beneath my bed.

It laid there. A stark, vibrant reminder that what had happened was real. The wires were real.

I pressed hard against my skin in various spaces on my body, but I found nothing. I tried my best to be discreet. If blondie was real, then so were the men. And if the men were real, they were watching.

It awakened something in me. An inner turmoil. A realisation that my life has been a lie. No genuine memories and until now, no drive to question it. I was a puppet who wanted desperately to sever the strings.

Regardless of my newfound consciousness, I still found myself at a bar within hours of discovering blondie's panties, checking out the talent.

Just as I was supposed to.

Is free will some sort of sick cosmic joke? I tried to fight a deep primitive need, but it was futile. I wasn't even sure that I controlled my own mind. I felt a tension in the back of my head and raised my hand to it. The area was hot to the touch. *Is this what fear feels like?*

Thoughts jumbled. Words turned into flurries of nonsensical letters. I knew what I had to do.

I scanned the whole bar. I scoured the hot redhead in the corner who I was certain I would be taking home. And then I walked to the bathroom with my beer in hand.

It was empty, which was pretty convenient for me. I took the opportunity and entered a stall, locked the door and smashed the glass against the cubicle. I took a piece of the jagged glass and held it in front of me.

I took a few moments to decide, but I settled on my stomach. I lifted my shirt and pressed the glass shard hard against my skin. No blood came out. My worst fears were confirmed. Instead of blood there were sparks and instead of a person there were wires.

Armed with my newfound knowledge, I lowered my shirt and I left the bathroom calmly.

I returned to my space, the perfect position to eye fuck the redhead from afar. I was going to take her home for sure. I had learned so much in such a short time but in reality, there was only one clear and unavoidable truth.

I'm a fucking machine.

EVERYDAY CHARLOTTE'S MOTHER FORGOT TO COLLECT HER FROM SCHOOL

"I'm sure she's just driving and can't answer her phone, she'll be here any moment."

I tapped my fingers on the desk and shot a pitiful smile at the little girl opposite me. It was a hollow promise. We'd already been sitting there for so long it was getting dark outside. I'd already sent my teaching assistant home. What was the good in both of us suffering?

This wasn't new. Some days it was minutes but often it was hours; the only thing consistent about Charlotte's mother was her ability to forget she had a daughter.

Charlotte was a bright child and a pleasure to teach. I couldn't understand why everything seemed to be so against her.

The other kids were cruel to her, leaving her out of games and group activities. I'd tried gentle, private words with kinder members of the class, encouraging them to include her. They all said no.

They said she was a witch.

Children can be evil. You really get to see that when you teach the little crotch goblins. They were eight years old and already ostracising someone weaker, even going so far as to infer she was some sort of monster. How cruel.

It made me really sad. The poor girl just couldn't catch a break. It was like no one wanted to be around her; she was a magnet forcing itself to the wrong end of another magnet.

She repelled.

"It's ok Miss Tackett. I know she isn't coming."

Charlotte stared blankly at the desk in front of her. She hadn't bothered to put her coat on, she was that conditioned to expect being forgotten. Her legs swung lightly back and forth below it.

"Of course she's coming Charlotte, your mother loves you… she's, uh, just very busy."

That was a half lie. I couldn't definitively prove that Charlotte's mother loved her, and it certainly didn't seem that way sometimes. She would arrive late but unconcerned, almost reluctant to collect her child.

She looked haggard and tired, more so each time I saw her. She often looked like she hadn't slept in days. She was jumpy, anxious, and irritable. It was obvious she needed help, that she was struggling.

I tried not to judge her, but it was hard. I sat with her forgotten child every day after that bell rang. How tired do you have to be to forget a child? Your only child.

And just like the other kids in the class, when Charlotte's mother would finally arrive, she looked at her as if she were some kind of monster.

"She doesn't love me."

I felt my heart drop. They were words you never wanted to hear a child say about their mother. They should all feel loved. Valued. The worst part was that she didn't even seem bothered, she was immune to it.

I remembered the time I'd tried to report to social services about Charlotte. My concerns seemed like nothing to them. The girl was fed, clean and always arrived on time. She wasn't withdrawn at school and didn't seem bothered by her lack of friends.

"We can't investigate a mother for lateness just because it irritates a school."

That was what the lady on the phone said to me. Then she hung up. I tried. I really did. I wanted so badly to help Charlotte, but I didn't know how to. I wasn't irritated by sitting with her like the social worker inferred, I just knew there was more to it. I could feel it.

"What makes you think that she doesn't love you?" I asked, desperate to draw out something that could help me help her.

"She's scared of me."

"What do you mean she's scared of you?"

"She locks her room when we get home, and she doesn't come out until it's time to take me to school." She answered nonchalantly, swinging her feet under the desk.

"Doesn't she make you dinner?"

"Of course Miss Tackett, she leaves it prepared on the kitchen side, all I have to do is eat it."

I thought of what an isolating existence that must be. To have no one to talk to all day and then go home to silence. What did Charlotte mean her mother was scared? What was her mother doing in that room?

"Does she have anyone in there with her?"

"No, Miss Tackett, she just stays in her room. She says it's the only way she's safe."

A lump formed in my throat. If she only felt safe in her room, then why didn't she keep her daughter in there too? *What was wrong with this woman?*

"Why wouldn't she be safe?" I asked, struggling to reel in my curiosity.

"Because I'm there. I told you she's scared of me."

Her words were jarring. It took me a few moments to compose myself. It was a baffling thought that anyone could be frightened of such a sweet young child.

"Why wouldn't she be safe with you? What does she think you'd do to her?"

"Because I'm a witch. She thinks I might hurt her."

Charlotte continued swinging her legs under the desk, her vacant state resident on her face. It broke my heart. I started mentally preparing a lesson on the effects of bullying.

She was so confused; she'd twisted up the cruel taunts and the abuse at home and started to consider herself a monster. It was devastating.

"Charlotte, you aren't a witch. You can tell me if the other kids are mean to you... I'll talk to them. Why do they call you that?"

I fought back tears. I'd thought that getting into teaching would be fun and fulfilling, but pupils like Charlotte were haunting. They worked their way into your thoughts long after that bell had rung.

"Because I broke Stephanie's arm, with my mind."

I was taken aback at her answer.

I remembered the incident she was referring to. It was early into the school year, and Stephanie tripped on the playground. She broke her arm in two places; it was nasty. A few other kids started a rumour that Charlotte had used her witch powers to do it.

They had all stopped standing near her outside after that, despite my protests and pleas. They'd hammered it in so hard that it was her fault that Charlotte started to believe it.

"Stephanie fell Charlotte. You didn't do it."

"I made her fall."

"*You don't have witch powers!* The other kids are just mean." I practically screamed, trying to contain my rage.

That was unprofessional. I know. I shouldn't have been discussing the other kids, and especially not my feelings on them, with the victim of their targeting. I couldn't help it, I just wanted to see her smile.

The rhythm of her swinging legs ground to a halt and she turned to face me, vacant eyes locked with mine and suddenly not so vacant anymore.

She laughed.

It was like the sound of nails running across a chalkboard slowly, dragged out to prolong the torture. It wasn't a child's laugh. It was something mocking, awful. I felt the sudden urge to walk out of the classroom and leave. Like everyone else in her life already had.

I couldn't explain where it came from. Had it come from her? Or did I imagine it? No. It must have been me. *She was a child.* I had to stop thinking like that.

"What if the other kids are right, though, Miss Tackett?" She asked sweetly, following that awful laugh.

"They aren't." I shook my head and composed myself. Charlotte's mother would be here soon, and I could talk to her about her daughter. Make her see how serious the situation was. I could help. "There's nothing wrong with you."

Charlotte's facial expression changed. She frowned, trying to process my words and what they meant to her. It didn't take long but I could see her calculating. Trying to work out whether she believed me or not. Maybe I was finally getting through.

Then it happened.

I felt a crunch. Out of nowhere I was struck by a searing pain in my arm. I felt parts of bone brush past each other as they snapped and jutted out of different points of flesh. I fell to the floor, screaming.

"I never said there was, Miss Tackett. I like being a witch."

She was doing this. A child. It was her.

"Charlotte, please stop!" I begged. "Your mother will be here any moment, please... please stop." I pleaded, desperate for her to stop hurting me.

Her eyes weren't so vacant anymore. They focused on me with laser precision, revelling in my realisation that I'd gotten it all so badly wrong.

I thought about how terrified her mother must have been. About how I hadn't listened to her classmates' concerns. All I'd ever seen was a victim. I was so wrong.

She looked at me writhing on the floor in agony, and she rolled her eyes. I felt my heart pounding so hard I thought it might burst through my flesh.

"She's not coming, Miss Tackett." Charlotte stood up from behind the desk and took a step towards the classroom door.

"What did you do!?" I panted, wondering if that poor, tired woman was out there. If she was in the car, and it was all just a cruel trick.

The little girl flashed me one more sinister grin as she exited the room.

"She isn't coming, Miss Tackett. My mother forgot to lock her door last night."

ARE YOU SITTING COMFORTABLY?

Do you ever imagine you're someone else?

That your life isn't your life, and that existence could be something more?

Do you walk down the street and imagine yourself walking in the shoes of interesting strangers?

Maybe you fantasise about being the sharply dressed, powerful looking woman that shares your train carriage every day. Maybe it's the insta-perfect couple, travelling the world with a picturesque smile, that take you to that dream place.

Maybe it's simple. Maybe you want money, a mansion, fame and a cool blue pool in an underground level of your own elegant compound. Maybe it's deeper than that. Maybe you want true love, food on the table, health and a happy family, nothing more, nothing less.

All these beautiful dreams that bring you comfort. They bring me comfort too.

When you dream do you dream of things being better? Do you wonder what it's like to have no worries? No stress. No pain. No misery.

Or do you dream of things being worse?

When you pass those interesting strangers in the street do you imagine the pinch of the sharply dressed woman's shoes, or do you imagine the water that seeps in the holes of the homeless man she passes battered trainers.

Maybe, instead of wondering what it's like to be that insta-perfect couple boarding a plane, you imagine how cold it is in the man's makeshift bed at the train station.

Maybe you wonder if that powerful looking woman is only dressed that way to retain some sort of value in a male dominated workspace. Maybe she detests everything about that immaculate red lipstick she sports.

Maybe you imagine that Instagram couple, travelling the world, scaling the side of a mountain, and plummeting thousands of feet to their deaths in the quest for a perfect viewpoint selfie.

I know I do.

I pass a lot of interesting strangers on my way to work and I wonder how it is to be all of them. The good, the bad and the ugly.

I walk and I visualise every diverse moment of the human experience.

I admire that sharply dressed woman.

I don't imagine it's easy to wake up every day and curate such a pristine image that early in the morning, but I'm sure the glass of artisan wine I picture her settling down with at the end of the night makes it worth it.

I admire another girl on my train as well.

She's younger and doesn't wear an immaculate layer of red lipstick, or any makeup at all. She dresses in a mint tunic, a traditional carers uniform. She's visibly tired, and she sometimes doesn't make it to the platform before the doors close.

She's trying... I can feel it. But there's no glass of artisan wine for her.

I admire her, but that doesn't stop me thinking of the human experience of the people she cares for. Wondering what it's like to be her... *and what it's like to be them.*

The people left in their own urine because their overworked carer missed the train. People lacking dignity, who can't leave their beds unaided so are left at the whim of that tired carers waning resilience.

That's not a comforting thought, is it?

It's not like the thoughts of mansions and gardens and cool blue pools. It's a stark reality that we push to the back of our minds because it makes us uncomfortable.

Are you sitting comfortably?

I bet some of you are. And I bet more of you aren't.

I pass these strangers every day on my journey to work and every day I wonder what it's like to be them. I wonder so hard that sometimes I can feel what they can, and thoughts of them follow me through the course of my own day.

They're like a haunting reminder that someone always has it worse.

Last week, that wondering hit a new level of intensity. I boarded my train, sat down opposite the sharply dressed woman, and suddenly I was her.

There was no fuzzy moment of body switching. No lights fading and waking dazed as another person. It was instant. I blinked and suddenly there I was looking back at me. An empty shell of a person on autopilot whilst I shared the woman's body.

It wasn't just a feeling I was imagining anymore; her pointed shoes pinched at her… my… feet and there was real, genuine pain. Not an emotional pang in the pit of my stomach, an actual cutting pain in my feet. Her shoes felt exactly as I expected.

Although I was there, she never left. She continued as if nothing had changed and I remained a silent passenger, living through the very day I'd envisioned hundreds of times.

I stared in wonder as we arrived at her workplace; an impressive, expansive office filled with well-maintained tropical plants. I smiled at the photograph of her and her two children that she picked up and kissed before logging on to her computer. I sighed at the barrage of emails she was met with when it loaded.

And I cringed in discomfort as her boss groped our leg.

As the day progressed, I realised that it wasn't all daisies for the sharply dressed woman. Amanda. That was her name. Known as mum by her kids, and Minxy Mandy by her lecherous boss.

Amanda applied her lipstick six times during the course of the day. Each time she looked in the bathroom mirror with a shame in her eyes. I felt that shame too. I felt everything she was feeling.

I knew that she was worried about reporting her boss. She was nearing forty and was already struggling to compete with the younger, more attractive talent. That was why she wore the red lipstick—she thought it made her stand out. That, and her ability to walk in crippling high heels and withstand the burning sensation they caused day in, day out.

At two o'clock she had to present to a boardroom filled with men who resembled her lecherous boss. She'd worked hard and was so certain they'd like it, but instead she was berated and humiliated for her ideas. We fought back every tear.

It was three o'clock when she first opened the drawer she kept the vodka in. She had decanted it into a clear water bottle for discretion, but she couldn't hide from me. I felt the warmth as it tore down our throat, neat. I felt the wobble in our ankles as we tried to remain steady in those shoes all day. I struggled with the blurring of the words on the fancy computer screen.

And I felt the emptiness when we entered Amanda's beautifully presented home. Devoid of a family her husband took away because of her drinking.

We drank more to sleep. Much more. So much that I don't remember the moment our head hit the pillow, or if it was the sofa instead. I just remember how numb our feet felt before there was nothing but blackness.

I woke up the next day as myself. In the same bed to the same alarm that I always do. I wasn't hungover, and my feet felt fine as I pulled on my trainers and left my house. I wondered if my experience as Amanda had all been a dream, but I quickly realised it hadn't.

I settled on the train, avoiding eye contact with my sharply dressed acquaintance as if we had partaken in some sort of forbidden dalliance the night before. I tried to steady myself as the train doors shut and I settled into position, eyes planted on the window.

Then I saw her.

The carer. The one who was always tired. Running fruitlessly towards the now moving train. I shut my eyes in despair, a bubbling anticipation in my stomach of what was to come. Then I opened them to see myself in the window of the train that was pulling away.

Her feet burned. Not in the same way as Amanda's had, but like someone who had run for a long time. She must have snoozed her alarm, just one too many times, then desperately scrambled her way to the station.

There was a sinking feeling in the pit of our stomach that I thought was my own. What if this was life now? What if I only ever got to be myself for a short time and the rest of my life was spent feeling the brunt of other people's problems?

It wasn't my sinking feeling.

The sinking feeling belonged to Julia, the carer. The carer who sat twitching for an hour as she waited for the next train. The carer who was met with anger when she phoned her company to explain what happened. The carer that had pulled a double shift the day before and was so exhausted she could barely stand.

That day we were anxious and were reprimanded by families who were upset Julia was late. We were kicked, spat at and bitten by clients while just trying to do our job.

I had previously assumed that the carer had it much harder than the sharply dressed woman and in a way she did. Her day *was* harder.

But while I was a passenger in Julia's life, I witnessed moments of joy. Moments of pride and satisfaction and passion for supporting someone else. Moments where she and her client shared a knowing smile. I felt the bond of someone just doing their best, and another person entirely reliant on it.

My day with Julia was long, but just like with Amanda, I woke up in my own bed.

I felt a terror that morning. I didn't want to leave my house; I didn't want to spend a day as somebody else. I just wanted to be me. To be my own individual person, to have control of my own body and to not have to feel anyone else's misery. Who was I?

I left for work. But I spent my day in a cardboard box. It was raining and the box was soddened quickly, and the homeless man whose body I was visiting didn't have enough layers for protection.

His feet were sore.

They had been so wet and sodden for so long and had spent so much time in the same pair of trainers that they felt tight, like the skin was suffocating. There was a tickle in our throat that caused intense coughing at small intervals, and I was shocked at just how many people walked by.

His name was Michael.

Michael had previously been in the army. That's what he told some of the few people that stopped for him anyway. He told others that he'd just come out of prison and others that he had been kicked out of his home because of his sexuality.

Maybe all of that was true. Maybe none of it was. I decided that day that I didn't really care. All I knew was that Michael was suffering and our feet hurt so bad. Did it matter how he ended up where he was?

He spent his day fighting with his street neighbours and pulling together as much change as he could to buy a sandwich and a small amount of heroin.

When I settled into his sodden cardboard cocoon for the night, feeling the rush of the drugs coursing through our veins, I pondered as we stared at the star littered sky. Our feet were numb, just like Amanda's had been after all that vodka.

Was Michael in any less pain than Amanda? Was he in any less than Julia?

Is there anyone out there who isn't fucking suffering?

I woke in my bed. Just like I always do. I drew my curtains, blocked my door and covered up the television. I didn't want to share anyone's suffering anymore. I just wanted to wallow in my own misery.

I didn't call in sick at work, but they called me a few times. I didn't answer. Fuck my job. Does any of it even matter? Do we all just drone around struggling through hardships just to repeat the cycle until we die? Are any jobs, any lipstick, any train or any fucking shoes even worth it? Not enough of us get that cool blue pool anyway.

The only place left in my house that could show me the image of a person was my mirror.

I caught a glimpse of myself and I shuddered... you would too. The sharply dressed woman does, the homeless man does, and the tired looking carer gives me a pitiful grin whenever our eyes meet. I've gotten used to it. You do when you walk around with a scar like the one I have from the kettle that fell on me as a child.

A horrible accident. Nothing nefarious. In fact, in comparison to most of the human race I've had quite a nice life. A life with parents who loved me and friends who saw beyond my disability. The only thing that ever bothered me was the strangers gawking at me in the street.

I've spent so long being stared at that I learned to stare back. At first, I was trying to fight my anger. I wanted to humanise the people that made me so uncomfortable. Honestly, I wanted to make them uncomfortable.

But now I know that they already are. Now I know if you stare too hard or look too deeply into anyone's life that no one is truly comfortable. No one has it all. No one lives a life filled with only flowers and rainbows and joy.

Are you sitting comfortably? *I already know you aren't.*

MY WORST FEAR

"Mum, Joey won't let me have my doll back!"

"Joey, be nice to your sister." I replied half-heartedly, struggling to contain the niggling irritation I felt at my kids bickering at a time like this. I didn't care that they were small, couldn't they read the room?

I didn't look at them, I couldn't. Couldn't bear the things they reminded me of.

They were kids. They didn't understand why I didn't care about a doll at their father's funeral. Logically, I knew that, but sometimes it was just really hard to accept.

I was *embarrassed.*

Wrangling my children while the entire church full of people looked at me with all that pity in their eyes. The good intentions were there but I felt patronised. None of them dared to speak to me, not even my own family. I couldn't blame them. What were they supposed to say? *The poor grieving widow.*

That's all I'd ever be now.

It was still raw. It had only been two weeks since the accident. I could still feel the injury I'd sustained to my spine.

Can you call it an accident? *That man may not have meant to murder my husband, but he meant to drink every drop he did before he got in the car.*

Drunk driver. A tragic accident. What if that tragic accident was *your* whole world? Ben... Ben and the kids were my whole world.

I was in the car too when that sack of breathing shit hit us. I barely remember the hours after, the doctors said I was in shock and they hid so much from me. It hurt, like I'd swallowed knives. It took them hours to even tell me Ben was dead.

I spent nights in the hospital after it happened, wishing I'd died instead.

I resented my mother when she came to see me the day I was discharged... why did she bring the kids? I wasn't ready to parent again yet. Wasn't that obvious? I'd just had so much ripped away.

"You need to do something Kel, think about your kids. Those two little angels are the only things that will get you through this." She managed between sobs.

How selfish. How fucking selfish.

She dumped those two insensitive little creatures on me, full of curiosity and questions, while I tried to quietly grieve their dad. She didn't even say goodbye to them, just left them there. Needy little parasites.

I hated my mum for it, but she was right. *I needed them.*

I spent the next few nights just watching them sleep. I never looked at their faces, I couldn't; but their little hands, their feet, their breathing chests, it kept me calm. I lived in their bedrooms.

Watching them breathe was a distraction, a soothing way to remind myself that *something* near me was alive.

Sometimes I could see Ben there too, smiling at me from across the strewn-out toys on the floor. It was the only time I felt any peace, just watching them sleep and trying to piece together the fragments of the accident.

It was such a blur. A blur of Ben; driving us home from the restaurant, his panic as he put his foot on the breaks and the other car hit from the side, the chaos the impact caused in our tiny metal shell.

Ben. Head back. Dead.

It was my worst fear realised, a part of me stolen. Or was it?

I'd become a bag of nerves, barely able to function. Every time I thought that I could breathe, even just for a short moment, that car was coming towards us again. The sound of the impact rang in my ears. It was never complete, always just those same tiny, terrifying fragments.

I watched as my daughter Jade's chest rose and fell gently. She was only six years old. She would barely remember her father. Neither would her tiny brother Joey, only four years old, in the next room.

Raising them alone. Without my soulmate. Was that my worst fear?

I flitted from room to room. Just watching my children and desperately avoiding sleep. Sleep bought dreams. Dreams I wasn't ready to see. Would I close my eyes and see Ben... the version of him I wanted to remember?

Or would I shut my eyes and see his corpse... neck lulling about in the driver's seat... trickle of blood dripping from the end of his nose... *BANG*.

NO. I wasn't ready to sleep yet. Not ready to see it.

I didn't make the children go to school. Who would? They didn't bat an eyelid at the change in routine. It was like their dad hadn't even existed. We spent those two weeks in a bubble of grief; them bickering over that stupid doll.

I found their dad too painful to mention, and they never once asked for him. I found that painful too.

Had they already forgotten him? Would they forget me too? *Was that my worst fear?*

The funeral was planned quickly. I thumbed through catalogues of floral tributes while the kids bickered in the background, interrupting me at every heart wrenching turn.

"Mum, Joey won't let me have my doll back!"

That doll. That stupid fucking doll. I'm sure I'd heard Jade say that same line a thousand times. Why were kids so repetitive? How could they be so *bothered* by something so *trivial?*

When she repeated it, on the pew during the funeral, after I'd told Joey to be nice, I snapped. I couldn't take it anymore. The constant bickering was exhausting.

"Will you both stop it! Your father is dead! Can't you see all these crying people?!"

The church stopped in a collective gasp. I felt that unwavering pity and it terrified me. Would I forever be ostracised? Was my worst fear becoming a charity case in the eyes of all my peers?

A monument to Ben. Maybe.

Ben's mother started to approach me. I'd avoided her since his death. Every phone call, every time she knocked on the door. I couldn't bear to look at her.

The same way I couldn't bear to look at the kids I'd just screamed at so publicly. The ones who just lost their dad. Frozen, snot drooling down my face, I was a mess.

"Kelly..." Ben's mum was crying. They all were. *Everyone* was sad, so why was there so much pity directed at me?

Most had taken a step back. Too uncomfortable to comfort the grieving widow, but not uncomfortable enough not to stare. I just didn't understand. I hated being the centre of attention.

Maybe that, selfishly, was my worst fear?

I backed away a little in my seat, careful not to go too far and crush my already traumatised children. They were close behind me.

I needed to be able to watch them breathe that night, watch their tiny chests rise and fall under the duvet. To know that I wasn't alone. Ben's mother took a seat on the other side of me.

Her face was etched in sympathy. Condescending, regretful sympathy, and genuine concern. She cared. I felt a pang of guilt for freezing her out. I moved to the side so she could see her grandchildren. Ben's children. They were right behind me.

"Kelly, I know you're in shock, but you need help. You know they're gone don't you... all of them?"

That was ridiculous. They were right there. Bickering. Right fucking there.... Wait... no. My eyes darted around the cavernous room, hovering at breaks in the lights and chaos.

There was more than one coffin in the room.

"Just because you lost your child doesn't mean you have the right to insinuate-" I bit back, but as I did an awful thought crawled from the depths of my mind. The depths of my memory.

Those other coffins were so small.

I turned, but this time I didn't see my children fighting over a doll, dressed in black on a church pew. This time I saw them, fighting over that same doll in the back of our family car, strapped into their little car seats.

The kids were in the car. They were right behind me.

I blinked, but the memory was too strong. I couldn't will myself back into that church no matter how hard I tried. I was stuck.

Stuck in the front seat of the car. On *that* night.

We'd gotten strapped in, just after the trip to the restaurant. The children were bickering, and I was fed up. Ben couldn't stop smiling. He never could. That man was just so damn content.

Why couldn't I have been the same? Why couldn't I have just listened to that bickering and heard the same blissful bird song that Ben did whenever our kids made a sound? Why was that damn bickering all I could hear?

"Mum, Joey won't let me have my doll back!"

They were the last words I heard before the impact. In an instant I was catapulted back into that vast empty church. Alone on the pew with the mother of my dead husband.

Grandmother to my dead children.

Suddenly my own mother's comments about my two little angels made sense. The pity made sense. The repetition of that fucking line about the doll made sense.

It was never Jade, it was me, desperate to remember.

I hadn't been able to see it before; the accident was so blurred. I was grieving. I didn't want to believe it, but now it was clear.

My children were right behind me. They were right behind me during the accident and they *died*.

I thought about it. Hard. I tried to process a million emotions at once as I stared at their tiny coffins. Was this whole situation my worst fear? You'd think so wouldn't you. Isn't it yours?

I took a deep breath as mourners left the hall. I tried to scramble to my feet, to walk out and prepare for life without them. A miserable existence on my own. Just as I turned to exit the row I was shaken by a little voice.

"Mum, Joey won't let me have my doll back!"

I turned to see them both, stood there in the same clothes they'd word in the restaurant. Except they were dirtier... torn... *bloodied*. I blinked, but they wouldn't go away. They followed me to their graves, and they followed me home.

I've tried everything and they're still there as I write this, right now, bickering over a doll.

I was wrong. About my worst fear. It was never that the kids *were* right behind me.

My worst fear is that they always will be.

SNAPCHAT FILTERS

Avery. Where do I even start with Avery?

My beautiful little sister. She was an adventurer growing up, who loved nothing more than climbing trees and making forts with twigs in the back garden. I'd kill to have her back the way she was. How we were. My little sidekick, ready to conquer mountains and anything else life threw at us, together.

We fought, but as far as sisterly relationships go, we did okay. She was my annoying best friend.

Then she grew up. It was like I missed it completely. I'm five years older and by the time I was leaving secondary school she was starting. I suppose I'd just been wrapped up in my own teenage dramas, enthralled with friends and dissociated from my family. But one day, out of nowhere, Avery was a teenager and the sister I knew was dead.

It started small, a valiant battle over a tube of mascara and hours of pleading for a phone, just like all her friends. Soon mud pies and conquering the mountain didn't matter and couldn't compare to sleepovers with the girls and perfectly posed selfies.

That was what really started to get out of hand. The selfies. It sounds ridiculous, but in this modern age that's the type of shit you have to worry about. Not staying out past curfew or bunking off school; they were archaic problems replaced by internet trolls and body dysmorphia; stemming from competing for imaginary thumbs up on the internet.

It was sad. I remember the days of MSN but damn was I glad I missed out on the days of snapchat.

Avery's generation got the worst of it. I remember the tears my sister shed when some young cretin commented "fat lol" on a selfie she'd posted. Two three-letter words were enough for my sister to starve herself for a week, to wreck her confidence.

I watched her change. She did whatever she could to stay in with the popular crowd. She craved attention, adoration and most of all, likes. She rarely conversed with us, opting to spend her time alone in her room, putting on a full face of makeup just to take a single picture.

I passed my a levels and went off to university. I left my loving parents and my self-absorbed sister behind and went to study. It's awful, but I didn't think about Avery all that much. She was fifteen years old and at the height of teenage ignorance, she didn't want to catch up with her older sister. Instead, I kept up with her through snapchat.

Every day she would post a dozen pouting pictures. All using those ridiculous filters. My least favourite of them all was the one that came with the black and white dog ears. Every photo those ears sat perfectly on her artificially smoothed face. After the first term, I'd pretty much forgotten what my sister really looked like.

I stayed at school over the break. Maybe things would've been different if I'd gone home and checked on my family, but I didn't. I'm ashamed to say that I didn't see any cause for alarm.

During the next term I took more notice of Avery's snapchat stories. What had started as montages of happy selfies and group photos with her friends became the same posed pout, in her bedroom, every time.

I don't mean that Avery reposted the same picture every time. The differences were subtle; clothes, hair, eyeshadow; but the pose and the position were the same. And so was that fucking dog filter. Despite the fake covering, I could see in my sister's digitally enlarged eyes that she wasn't happy. Something was going on.

The day I called my mother was the first I'd spoken to her in two weeks. I hadn't been great at communication since I left, but that morning Avery had posted another photo and I was sure I could see her crying, even if her eyes were as blurred as the rest of her skin.

"You have no idea how bad it's been, Alice; she never leaves her room. Last week she stopped coming down for dinner.

"She climbs out of her window late at night. I've gone to check on her before and she isn't there. I've called the doctors, mental health teams, the school but no one's helping and she won't budge."

My mum sounded utterly defeated. My parents had been strict but fair and always tried their best for us. It broke my heart to hear her so crushed. It broke my heart even more to think of the adventurer I watched grow up, reduced to taking sad selfies alone in her bedroom.

I got the next train home. I had to send a few grovelling emails to lecturers, but I managed to get extensions on my papers. I needed to know that Avery was ok.

I couldn't imagine the utter terror on my parents' face when I walked through the front door. I expected a warm embrace, a welcome home for the daughter who had been gone for six months. But I suppose I was entirely more present than the one living there.

It was strange not to see Avery come bounding down the stairs. My parents just looked at me, lost for words.

"What's happened? Is she ok?" I asked, dropping my bags in the entrance hall.

"It's gotten worse the past few days, Alice. She's barricaded herself in the room and she's refusing to come out. Something's… something's wrong with her voice." My dad managed as my mum sobbed into his shoulder. "Paramedics are on their way, but there's a three hour wait for an ambulance at the moment. She's conscious so they can't prioritise her."

"What's wrong with her voice?"

Dad looked at the ground, poorly avoiding the question, and mum struggled to breathe through sobs, hands shaking. I shared a look with them before charging up the stairs.

"Avery! Open up. I'm home, aren't you gonna come and say hi?" I rapped on the door loudly with my knuckles. Nothing.

"AVERY! Open." I tried, a little louder.

I… missed you. A voice answered.

It was a voice that I didn't recognise; lispy and laboured, like a person trying to talk and chew on food. I felt a deeply uncomfortable chill run through my entire body. Who the fuck was in my sisters' room? And if it was her, what the fuck had happened?

"Come on Avery. Mum said you'd been sneaking out… meeting boys?" My voice wobbled in fear as I desperately tried to cling to some normality. Our mothers' sobs punctuated my words and filled the gravid silence.

I had to find the perfect one.

The vile, unrecognisable voice was responding cryptically. I was almost certain the perfect one hadn't been referring to a boyfriend. I felt the urge to get away, to get the train back to school and forget about my sister. Unbelievable what a little fear can do to a person. They say we all have fight-or-flight responses and that day I learned I'm a flyer. It took everything I had not to run.

I sat downstairs with my parents, dutifully waiting for the ambulance to come. I wondered if it would, or if the operator had written off the worried parents, making jokes with colleagues about a teenager who wouldn't leave her room. I would've laughed too if I heard it. But I knew that something was seriously wrong.

I don't know why it didn't click sooner. I'd even spoken with "Avery" about her late-night rendezvous, but around an hour into my arrival I remembered the trellising at the back of the house. Her entire means of escape.

"Just wait for the professionals. They'll be here!" My dad called up as I placed my first foot on the lower portion.

"And what if it's not her? Then we need to call the police too! That didn't sound like my sister, we need to know!" I answered, not really requiring any response at all as I clung on to gaps in the latticed wood. A few meters and I was at her window.

There she was, my sister, sat on the end of her bed facing the window with her head down. Just like in the pictures.

It had been so long since I'd seen a filter-less picture of her that it took me a moment to notice the crude stitches joining her face to the floppy, bloodied, black and white dog ears that expertly mimicked the ones in her photos. Suddenly I realised what she meant by finding the perfect one.

I almost fell from the trellising as she raised her head to reveal her eyes, missing the lower lids in an attempt to enlarge them. Despite the horrors, she sported her signature vacant expression and pout, smothered in red lipstick. She was barely there, just posing in front of me with her disfigured face.

I felt the bile rise in my stomach and sweat form on my palms, making it hard to hold on. Avery looked me dead in the eyes as a tear escaped, turning crimson as it mixed with the blood lining her eye wounds. She didn't say a word and the pout didn't move. The sight was shocking, but it didn't explain the voice that I had spoken to through the door. So I asked the only question I could think of in the moment.

"Avery, why?"

She took a breath in through her nose and opened her mouth to answer. As soon as her lips parted a long and grotesque, rough dog tongue unravelled, barely stitched to her own, lulling beneath her chin. The tongue was gangrenous and necrotic tissue barely clung to the sewn thread.

I just wanted to look like my pictures.

BLENDED FAMILIES

My mum died. It's been a while now, but it still feels weird to say those words. Or even to type them.

People avoided asking me about it, so I never really got to say it out loud; I suppose cancer is a fucking awkward topic, sure to bring down any mood. Instead, they just threw pity at me with their eyes and avoided conversation of death and sickness all together.

I spent a year on eggshells. I couldn't understand it when my dad told us he'd met someone new. How had he found the time? We were still being treated like those little orphan kids and he'd managed to date. I'd be lying if I said I wasn't a bit angry.

My little brother Sven was too young when she died to understand what we were going through. He was barely out of nursery and still couldn't grasp that mummy wasn't coming home. I wasn't sure what was worse, having years with her and losing her, or avoiding the pain by being too young to remember.

Meanwhile, I was stuck with what felt like a grief tumour, attacking every part of my body as aggressively as the one that killed my mum. Along with a pile of university entrance exams, all in the same month. I buried my mother one day and sat advanced mathematics the next.

I made it to university. My dad was shocked. I know he expected me to fail. He had the same pity eyes that all the other kids at school did. I was grateful for the fresh start and a chance to flee all those haunting, painful memories. And I took it. Anything to be more than just the girl whose mum died.

I weathered the summer, dealing with the grief and the misery in my home, only relieved by Sven's infectious giggles. I was going to miss them regardless of the pain, but still, I packed up my car and moved miles away when September hit.

Every visit home I felt the eggshells pricking at my feet. A week here and there, then straight back to my uni bubble, where I could be someone else. The year passed so quickly. As selfish as it may sound, I detested my visits home. But none more than the start of this summer, a year on, when my dad announced his new woman, my mother's replacement.

Her name was Ally, and she had a fifteen-year-old daughter named Violet. My dad hadn't planned to tell us so soon, but he was left with no choice when Ally was evicted just before the government lockdown, leaving her and her kid homeless. We learned about our new stepfamily only three hours before they moved into our home.

He begged us to give them a chance. Sven, only six years old at the time, was on board. I was tougher, but I didn't put up a fight, instead opting for a frosty, unfeeling demeanour.

"Some stepfamilies do really well Taylor, please just give them a chance. We might all get on and work as a blended family."

I remember him saying that and thinking that he must have read some books and articles on "blended families", trying to make himself sound clever. I thought about what a ridiculous term that was. I recognise now that he was trying; I wish I'd given him more credit for it, but at the time I barely hissed in response and waited in silence until they knocked on the door and our lives changed forever.

I wish I could lament my dad's choice of woman, but Ally was beautiful. She had a soft and nurturing face and a voice that could read bedtime stories. She was kind, patient and made every respectful and non-invasive effort to befriend my brother and me. I completely got the attraction and I saw how happy she made my dad.

Bitter as I was, Ally was never the problem. Violet was.

I knew it the moment they walked through the door. A perpetually sour faced young girl with something slightly intimidating about her. Where Ally radiated light, Violet was there to suck it up. When she wasn't looking sour, she had a smug grin that she tried to hide by pursing her lips, and she made no effort to converse at all. I couldn't put my finger on it at first. I assumed it was nerves, but by that night she'd proven my reservations correct.

I retreated to my room pretty soon after an awkward dinner. Ally had tried to keep the conversation flowing, but none of us were ready to open up yet. You could hear even the faintest clink of a fork hitting a plate.

My bedroom was opposite the bathroom and around 9pm I started to smell my mother.

That sounds odd, but it's true. My mum always wore the same perfume; it was distinctive and bought tears to my eyes as it seeped under the gap in the door. It's strange that things like a scent can spark that kind of emotional reaction, but I was a mess.

I stumbled out of the room rubbing my eyes and flung open the bathroom door where the smell was coming from. There she was.

Violet.

Holding the half empty bottle of my dead mums' perfume that had previously sat on the window ledge next to a framed photograph, she spritzed it at herself again before turning to face me. There wasn't a human on earth that wouldn't have seen it was sentimental.

Her eyes lingered on mine for a moment and she pursed her lips, attempting to conceal another telling smile. After a few seconds of eye contact she dropped the bottle and screamed, as if I'd made her jump.

The room, hallway, and every upstairs carpet of my house saturated with that strong aroma as the bottle smashed. It was the kind of smell that would take months to eradicate entirely. Ally and dad ran to our aid, suspecting the worst.

I saw the relief and heartbreak in his eyes when he saw what happened. I tried to explain. I said she'd done it on purpose, but she insisted she didn't know and only dropped it because I startled her. She couldn't have been more apologetic. I have to admit, Violet played innocent well, but I saw straight through her.

My protests were ignored and the whole thing was explained away like an innocuous accident.

"I'm sorry, Taylor still struggles with... you know." I heard my dad say to Ally in the hall, when they thought I was already asleep. Violet had stolen a piece of my mum and made me look insane all in one action.

That was only night one.

The incidents with Violet continued. It started small, dropping a vase, knocking salt into an almost finished pan of food and overwatering a plant, all sorts of clumsy mishaps.

Then things escalated. About a week into our venture as a *blended family,* Violet created the type of havoc that doesn't go unnoticed.

I was studying at the table in the kitchen and Ally had been cooking. She left with a pot of potatoes boiling on the stove and asked me to keep an eye on them while she showered. I didn't think much of it. I watched and adjusted the flame accordingly as the water bubbled and expanded.

When Violet entered I barely noticed. I'd tried to avoid her at all possible cost after the perfume and I wasn't about to stop. I didn't look round, make eye contact, or do anything to attract her attention.

I listened as she walked to the fridge, opened the door, and took a swig of juice, all while still focusing on the potatoes. If I'd have just looked, been more wary, I'd have noticed her turn and seen her lips pursed, hiding the same smug, sinister smile as before.

As she turned, she plunged her hand into the pot of boiling water.

I screamed. In shock and pain at the molten, flying droplets that kissed my skin. She didn't. I'd never seen anything like it. She almost looked like she was enjoying her skin melting and bubbling as I looked on in horror.

"What are you doing?!" I cried, before begging her to stop. I threw a hand around her upper arm and tried to wrench it out of the pot but she wouldn't move an inch. She was planted.

"Time for dinner, sis!" she responded with glee.

I fought with her like that for a while, desperately trying to stop her as the smell of her boiling flesh battled my mum's spilled perfume that had permeated the walls days before.

Then Ally walked in.

Immediately Violet started wailing, like you would expect from a person whose hand was sizzling and blistering in liquid. Tears streamed from her dead, blue eyes as she started to repeat a single word.

"STOP STOP STOP STOP STOP!"

I saw what she was trying to do, and it was genius. It looked so bad, me clutching the same arm that was stuck in the pot. Ally looked stunned and disturbed as I let go and backed away. Violet pulled out her hand, melted almost to the bone, and dropped to the floor, screeching in agony.

I stood in the corner near catatonic, back to the wall as Ally dialled the ambulance. My new step mum didn't make eye contact with me, not once, as she tended her spawn on the floor. The three minutes the ambulance took felt like a lifetime with me silent in the corner and the smell of death filling every inch of the room.

When my dad got home from the store with Sven, I told him what happened. He didn't give me a chance to explain or to try and convince him that Violet was the literal devil. He didn't comfort me; instead, he left my six-year-old brother in my care and fled to the hospital to be with his new family.

I wondered if he suspected Violet too. If he thought I did it, then why would he leave me with Sven? But if he thought I didn't do it, then why would he go to her? I waited for police sirens all night, to pick me up for my evil crime.

They never came.

At the break of dawn, still awake, I watched my dad's car pull into the drive, two people in the passenger seats. Ally walked Violet upstairs, bandages up to her elbow, and settled her in her room, the old spare.

My dad sat opposite me in the living room, eyes brimming with tears, and shushed me before I could say a word. I felt my heart pound as Ally's footsteps made their way back down the stairs. I wasn't worried about my fate; I was worried about my little brother being in such close proximity to that monster. I had no idea what Violet was capable of.

Ally walked into the room and rushed towards me. I braced myself for a slap, a punch, some kind of attack, but instead she embraced me, pulling me in close so she could whisper in my ear.

"I saw everything. I'm sorry. There's something wrong with her."

I felt a rush of relief go through my entire body as I communicated with my dad and Ally using nothing but our eyes. I was so incredibly grateful; they were as scared as I was.

"You need to call a doctor." I pleaded with Violet's mother, not only concerned for myself but for anyone who could do what Violet did without so much as a genuine flinch.

"This isn't something any doctor can fix, honey. I'm so sorry. We can't talk about this here, let's sit outside."

The three of us moved to the patio in the back garden, Ally taking special care to ensure every window to the back of the house was closed, terror in her face. I couldn't imagine being scared of my own flesh and blood, but Ally's fear was incomprehensible.

"She's done this before Taylor. I thought we were past this, but I was wrong. I promise I never would have put your family at risk if I'd thought for even one second that..."

"What do you mean, *past* this? Her hand wasn't fucked up before."

"I don't mean that particular stunt, I've never seen her do anything so brazen before. I mean the little things, all those evil malicious actions that you can't quite prove. I've suspected her for a long time, she wasn't the same after her dad died."

"If you think something's wrong then why can't you take her to a doctor honey." My dad cut in. "I can't have my kids at risk."

As grateful as I was that my dad was standing up for us, I could see the sheer, unadulterated horror on Ally's face, and I couldn't help but pity her. How many smashed bottles of perfume had she lived through?

"You don't get it Joe. I did. I took her to the doctor. She had three appointments, each time the doctor flagged more concerns than the last."

"What happened to her?" I asked.

"She hung herself." Ally replied facing the ground, sombrely.

"It isn't Violet's fault that the woman was disturbed. We need to try again, call someone new." my dad's voice shook as he spoke. But ever the optimist, he tried to offer comfort.

Ally laughed a humourless, soulless laugh.

"It isn't that simple. She didn't just die. She hung herself while in session with Violet. I wasn't in the room, but I saw my kid's face when I picked her up and honestly, it wouldn't surprise me if my daughter tied the noose. No emotion would've been easier, but she looked delighted."

I felt a chill run down my spine.

"Did you report her to the police?"

"Yes."

"And what happened?"

"I finally saw what kind of monster she is. They came to question her, and I left to make tea... give them a little privacy. I still thought at the time there was a chance I was imagining it."

She started to cry softly. I hadn't known her for long, but I desperately wanted to give Ally a hug. If it weren't for Violet, she would've been a welcomed addition to the household. My dad placed an arm around her and she continued.

"She just looked at them. I can't prove a thing, but I know she did it. She squinted and their bones cracked. Blood poured from every opening and they died on my couch. As they lay there, she told me I shouldn't have called them."

"What the fuck Al? Why didn't you say anything?" My dad was angry, but more worried than anything. I could hear the compassion in his tone.

"How are you supposed to admit that you don't think your child's human? We ran. Years passed and nothing else happened... meeting you, moving here. I started to wonder if the whole thing had been a sick nightmare until last night."

"Well, it's not a nightmare, so what do we do?" I begged, needing some kind of viable solution to the literal demon lying mere feet from my young brother.

"We keep her happy. She didn't want to go to therapy. She didn't want to move here. If we get her used to it... if we just make everything ok, she'll settle... she has to. I fear there isn't another choice."

I watched my father squirm at the prospect of sharing his home with a powerful and presumably evil entity. He knew there was another choice. He could yeet the pair of them to the curb, but I knew that he wouldn't. We may have only just learned about Ally, but they were in love. Anyone could see that. I can't say it was a situation I'd ever envisioned us as a family being in.

I'm sure he hadn't either.

I tried to sleep that morning but all I got was a few broken hours. Every knock, bump, and creek in the house had me on edge. I opened my Sven's door and peaked inside more times than I could count.

A whole two weeks passed like that. Every noise, every night, every dinner, we were on edge. All of us but Violet. Even Sven picked up on the negative energy. She... *it*... enjoyed the psychological torture. She loved watching us tiptoeing around her, bowing to her every whim. It wasn't like when my mum died and I had to walk on eggshells. Living with Violet was like walking on rusty nails.

She's tormented me for months. Every time we were alone she made that pursed lipped smile. She ran her fingers across the cold stove to taunt me and I'm not sure if it was the trauma or Violet, but every time I was certain I could smell her necrotic, burning flesh.

The ever-changing bandages and pus-filled blisters that seeped out the gaps were a constant reminder. If she caught me cringing, she would wink and laugh.

Violet and I had very few verbal interactions. Whenever I was unfortunate to have to communicate with her she would call me *sis*. Just like she had as she plunged her hand into the water. It made my skin crawl. Her voice was high pitched and full of malevolent joy. It may have passed as happy to a very small child, but to anyone with emotional maturity could hear straight through it.

Still, despite the unease and the drawn-out misery, there were no further incidents. Ally insisted she knew what she was doing whenever we caught a stolen whisper in the halls. Things didn't get better, but they did get easier to bear. There was even the occasional smile in the home.

Sven's infectious giggle cut through the dark atmosphere whenever it could.

I hadn't expected to be home as long as I was. The lockdown lasted longer than expected and I lost out on loads of time at university. Everything that had happened with Violet made the idea of going back harder, but I knew that September was looming. So yesterday I drove back to my dorm to drop off half my stuff and make the move back easier.

I crashed there for the night and had the best sleep I'd experienced since returning home. I thought about Dad, Sven and Ally. All of them stuck there with that *thing* while I got to escape for the night. I felt selfish, but I was glad. Just one night away from the misery.

This morning my life changed again. I could feel it coming up to the driveway. Something was incredibly wrong.

There wasn't a thing out of place; dad's car sat on the drive and the flowers bordered the garden like they always had. The house had always been so pretty. Its quaint exterior hid the evil inside so well.

I turned my key in the door and took a tentative step inside. I can't explain why I felt so uncomfortable. In truth, I had felt uncomfortable for months, but there was something more to it this morning. I saw her the moment I entered.

I walked through the hall, past the living room door and to the kitchen in a trance, without even stopping to drop my bags.

Violet sat at the table, blue eyes fixated on me and lips pursed, hiding a smile. In front of her were two glasses filled with a dark orange, smoothie like liquid, decorated with blood orange slices and finished with a tiny paper umbrella. It sat next to a chopping board and a blender, spattered inside with pulp. She looked sinister as ever, but the drinks actually looked pleasant.

She slid one towards me.

"Hey sis, I missed you and it got me thinking about how I want us to get along better, take a seat."

She gestured to the seat opposite and without taking my eyes off her for a single second I sat down, heart pounding.

"Where is everyone?" I asked, trying to stay calm and willing the beads of sweat forming on my face to stop.

"They're all in the living room. This is time for just me and you, sis. Have a drink."

I looked at the cup and back at Violet. I wondered if I shouted, would they come running? It was far too quiet. Sven was never that quiet, and it was far too late for him to be sleeping. She parted her lips gently to giggle. Her giggle sent a quiver through every bone, vein, and tendon in my body.

"You think it's poison, don't you?"

"Would you blame me?"

Her smile turned to a scowl and she snatched the drink back, taking a swig of it and then another of hers. She made a gross, sloshing, satisfied noise, savouring the flavour.

"See, just paranoia, sis. I don't think you've been very fair to me. Try it, I made it just for you and I'm going to be very offended if you don't."

My hand shook as I reached out for the glass. My entire being was telling me not to, but instinct was being overridden by mental images of her hand melting and the police officers, bleeding from their eyes, nose and ears. Or maybe I never had a choice to begin with. At the time I know I hadn't properly considered that some fates are worse than death.

I took a sip.

An unexpected, indescribable and ghastly flavour filled my mouth, a gloopy texture with small, hardened shards swishing around my tongue. I turned to the floor and spat. It was the first time I'd taken my eyes off Violet since entering the house.

Now I realise that's exactly how she wanted it.

The floor was covered in blood, spattered in artistic patterns along the bottom of cabinets and across every tile. I turned to try and take in more of the house, noting the blood saturating the hallway carpet. I'd been so fixated on the monster I'd stepped straight through it before.

Steadying myself on my chair, I took another look at Violet, who had broken into full hysterical laughter. I thought of my dad, his lovely girlfriend and my gorgeous little brother, knowing I wasn't going to see any of them again. Then I took another look at the cup.

It didn't take long to put two and two together. The bile in my stomach had already made it to my throat by the time she spoke, but still, her next words will haunt me forever.

"What's wrong sis, don't you think our families blended well?"

MY FRIEND THE SCARECROW

The rural area I grew up in made the smallest towns appear densely populated. It was the sort of place where you had to cycle a mile or so to the nearest neighbour and the bus only came through twice a day.

Most kids think growing up on a farm is some sort of constantly thrilling adventure. The kids at my school in the nearest town certainly did.

They didn't see me waking up at four in the morning just to get ready in time for my parents to get me there, or how lonely weekends were when your friends lived so far away. No. They thought it was all just chickens and tractors. In truth, I resented it.

The farm was on a large plot of land. We had acres surrounding the house, ending at a thickly forested border that separated us from two distant neighbours and some fields.

My parents would let me play freely on the farm from a young age, my only rule was to stay on the land that we owned. Where the trees started, I should've always stopped.

Boredom was a killer; chickens aren't so exciting when they're your day-to-day life and there's only so much fun a kid can have on his own.

When I was about eight years old, I started to explore the woods that made up the border, at first weaving in and out of the trees on the edge of the farm and eventually building up the courage to go deeper into the forest.

I was careful, making sure that I embarked on my adventures almost as soon as I'd left the house so that I had maximum time to explore without being caught by mum and dad. The day I first made it through the border I was trying to time how long it took to walk through the trees.

It was fifteen minutes until I reached the clearing owned by Mr. Hinchcliffe, an elderly potato farmer to the left of us. He was known by the local people for being insular and quiet.

It was a large, circular clearing, cut off from the rest of his land by a different species of tree to the ones in the forest. It's like they had been planted years before to create and keep the clearing separate and hidden.

In the centre of the circle was a man stood facing me, unmoving. I was terrified at first, convinced that Mr. Hinchcliffe was about to March me home for trespassing. I tried to conceal myself behind a tree whilst keeping an eye on the man, realising that he hadn't moved an inch.

It took me a moment, but the poles eventually gave it away. That and the lack of feet—the figure started from the ankles. The man in the clearing wasn't a man at all, he was a scarecrow.

I was fascinated. I stayed behind my tree but strained my eyes to try to get a better look. My parents put scarecrows up around our own crops, but none of ours were ever as elaborate as the one stood in the middle of Mr. Hinchcliffe's clearing.

He was realistic, more realistic than anything that I'd seen before. He wore a red checked shirt, a straw hat, and had a wide smile stitched across his face from the corners of his lips. I wanted to get closer, but as I emerged from the trees, I could feel his eyes on me and could've sworn that I saw his fingers move.

I ran back through the woods to the farm, eager to get home and try to forget about what I'd seen, my little heart pounding. I didn't tell my parents about the scarecrow or the clearing, but as I laid in bed that night all I could think about was that smile, stitched across his face.

I spent hours that night convincing myself that scarecrows couldn't move. What I'd seen must have been the wind, I was just freaking out over nothing.

I tried to stop myself from going back, but I desperately wanted to get a closer look. I wondered what Mr. Hinchcliffe had used to make his scarecrow look so realistic, and my curiosity eventually got the best of me.

Three days after my initial discovery, I left the farm and made my way through the same dense section of woods until I reached the clearing again. I stopped behind the same tree, inspecting the scarecrow until I'd gathered the bravery to get a little closer.

Mr. Hinchcliffe's creation was even more spectacular up close. I couldn't work out what material he had used to make the face, it was like something out of a film. I touched the skin to try to understand what it was but I couldn't; it felt like my own, just colder. I was in complete awe.

The smile had been hand stitched into the skin-like material. It must have taken the old man hours. If the scarecrow had ever had feet, they had been buried in the dirt to help him stand. Poles were driven into the ground behind him and tied to his torso, keeping him propped up and secured.

The longer I looked at the scarecrow, the more I felt like he was alive in ways. I was certain that he occasionally blinked and that his chest rose and fell. I was cautious and more than a little unsettled, but I took my time and inspected him as much as I could.

Walking back to the farm through the forest, I couldn't get the scarecrow out of my thoughts. I struggled to make conversation over dinner, my mind filled with that stitched up smile.

I became obsessed. I returned every day for the next three weeks. The clearing became my place of solace and the scarecrow that stood there my best friend. I would sit by his planted ankles reading and drawing in my sketchbook.

I named the scarecrow Peter and I spoke to him whenever I could. I told him my deepest thoughts and feelings, cried to him when I was sad, and spent every moment that I could with him.

I was careful not to sit in the clearing for too long and always returned to the farm before my parents felt I was gone too long. I wished I could spend more time with Peter, it's sad when I think back to what a lonely kid I must've been to spend so much time with an object. A glorified effigy of a human.

With every visit, the rising and falling of Peter's chest lessened. I stopped catching him blinking and his skin started to sag and grey after a few days of rain. I knew it must just be me getting used to him, realising that he would never spring to life and answer me like a real friend, but it still made me a little sad.

After a while Peter's magic was gone, I would visit like always, but it didn't feel the same, the clearing was as empty as the rest of my life, and my propped-up friend in the middle was in a sorry state.

The stitched smile barely held itself in place, and lumps of the material that made up his skin had started to dry and fall off. He couldn't even scare the birds away anymore and often had multiple perched on his straw hat and shoulders, pecking at his face.

One day, towards the end of that summer, I made my way through the clearing to find it empty. Peter was gone. There wasn't a trace of him left bar the pole that still stuck firmly in the ground. Despite the fact that my initial fascination with Peter had already depleted, it still felt like a loss.

My parents couldn't understand why I was so withdrawn. I was grieving for someone that had never actually existed. Eight years old and I already understood what it was to mourn a friend.

I visited the clearing multiple times and it remained empty. School restarted and the autumn hit, bringing with it icy winds that would frost the entire land. I spent less time outside and barely visited Mr. Hinchcliffe's clearing through the winter.

By the time we reached the next summer, Peter and the time I'd spent with my silent friend were all but forgotten. It was by chance, on a sunny day, that I decided to walk through the woods one more time to my old sanctuary.

I didn't expect it; I thought that part of my life was over, but there she was. An entirely new scarecrow propped up just like Peter had been, ankles pressed firmly into the ground with poles behind her. She wore a different outfit, dungarees and a yellow checked shirt, but the straw hat was unmistakably the same.

Her chest rose and fell gently just like Peter's once had and her eyes appeared to move barely millimetres as I looked into them. It was almost impossible to see, but I was sure that she was alive.

She gave me hope that I wouldn't have to spend a summer lonely and sad on the farm. Her stitched smile gave me the same familiar, comforting feeling as a hot chocolate on a chilly night.

The process repeated, just like it had with Peter. As the weeks passed, she looked more haggard and less alive. The magic became less, the loneliness returned and eventually, she disappeared entirely.

Every year would be the same. Summer would come and with-it Mr. Hinchcliffe would build a new scarecrow. They came in every age, shape and gender. A new friend that I knew would wither and vanish just like the others. Regardless, I grew attached to every single one of them.

As I got older and my parents awarded me more freedom I could spend more time in the town, with friends that spoke back. After a while I started to forget about the scarecrows entirely, favouring girls and nights out to sitting with inanimate objects.

Years passed by and I left home to take a degree in art. University changed my life, for the first time, I had a group of friends around me all the time. Ones that weren't planted in the ground. I moved in with them and only went home for Christmas.

I never forgot about Mr. Hinchcliffe's scarecrows, they were my lifeline for so long, but I did move on, I didn't need them anymore.

It's been three years since I last spent a summer on the farm and lock down has forced me back here. When my housemates all returned to their families, I couldn't bear the idea of just me in the house, so I did the same.

I wasn't intending to visit the clearing. In fact, it's been years since I really thought about it. I've been too wrapped up in a social life that I never had as a kid.

It was only when my mother bought up her new friend Linda, who now lives at the farm to the left, that I was reminded of my childhood secret. One that I now wish I could erase.

"What happened to Mr. Hinchcliffe?" I asked, my heart sinking at the sudden realisation that I would never get to see another one of his amazing creations. My mother hung her head, trying to plan a response.

"It was awful, Charlie, all over the local news. He stopped responding to his sister's calls last year and after a while she sent local police to do a welfare check.

"When they arrived, he wasn't in the house, so they started searching the land and they found him, collapsed in a wooded bit just the other side of our trees, he'd died of a heart attack."

"Why would that make the news?" I asked, a bead of sweat running down my neck as I imagined Mr. Hinchcliffe, dead in the clearing. *My* clearing. My mother's face somehow lowered further.

"He wasn't alone, Charlie. They found a woman strapped to a pole next to his body. He'd been injecting her with some sort of drug that kept her completely paralysed while conscious. He'd planted her feet in the ground to keep her upright and dressed her up like a... scarecrow.

"Police combed the land and found 45 bodies buried. He'd been at it for years."

I felt bile rising in my throat. My mind began connecting dots I'd never imagined.

"What happened to the girl?" I asked.

"She survived, barely. When they finally got her conscious, she wrote a letter explaining that she'd been strapped to that pole for two weeks before she was found. Hinchcliffe took every precaution possible to keep her alive up there.

"Worst of all, she can only communicate through writing now after what he did to her face. The sick fuck cut her mouth up, only to stitch it back into a smile."

THE MAN IN THE SHED

I remember the day I picked it up. It was flat, packed neatly in a box, with what felt like hundreds of tiny pieces and screws. All fitted together like Tetris.

I'd always wanted a shed. That sounds stupid, I know. But I'd lived in flats for years and now I'd moved I finally had a garden, some outdoor space and a place to put a shed.

I wanted to use it as an escape. Not a place for my tools, or for junk that I didn't want in the house. I wanted a haven that I could spend time in, somewhere I could hide from the world.

So when it arrived, flat packed in all its glory, I was ecstatic.

It took hours. I was only one petite woman and I struggled, but I didn't want to ask for any help. I was determined that this would be mine. Only mine. I didn't want to let anyone in on my project.

When it was finished, I stepped back and looked at my handiwork. I considered what type of chair I might like inside, whether I wanted books or a television and if I wanted to paint it or leave the wood.

I always struggled to make my own decisions.

The next morning I rushed out to buy it all. I filled my car with plush furnishings and paint cans, decorative pictures and a rug that was more than I could really afford.

I got home. I dumped it all in the house and began moving items to the shed. I started with the paint and rollers; I put them all in a tough bag and trudged across the glass to my private little haven.

And there he was.

There was a man in my shed. He wasn't anything special to look at, just a man, maybe a little younger than middle aged. He was handsome but tired. His face sagged as if he hadn't slept in weeks, and he was wearing a tattered suit and a pair of broken dress shoes.

"What are you doing here?" I asked, heart thumping as I dropped my bag and it split, paint can crashing and spilling across the grass.

"I don't much like that colour." He replied, gesturing to the duck egg blue stain across the lush foliage.

"Who are you?" I pushed. Frozen to the spot.

"My name's Eli. I came with the shed."

I didn't answer at first. I was busy coming to terms with the ridiculousness of his statement. People don't come with sheds. *You can't flat pack a person.*

"You need to leave." I answered, assessing the situation, wondering if he'd concealed a weapon and was going to attack me.

Would he force me into my house? Take my electrical items, my jewellery... *my clothes?* I stood in the garden staring into the shed in utter terror, blue spatter everywhere.

"You're mighty nervous, miss. I'm not here to hurt you, scouts honour."

"Were you a scout? How do I know you won't hurt me?" I wondered if he was homeless, using previous scouting skills to find shelter. I found myself inexplicably softening to his presence.

"Heavens no, can't join the scouts when you live in a box. I only know the box and now, this room. It's much more spacious in here."

I was baffled.

"You weren't in the box. I'm not stupid... please... please leave before I call the police."

"I wouldn't do that if I were you."

His tone was sinister, serious, and confident. My heart sunk. It wasn't the first time I'd heard those words. Not the first time a man had made me so frightened for my life that I threatened the police. I didn't have a leg to stand on before, but I wanted this time to be different. This time the haven was mine, *my private space.*

Yet still, in an instant, he held all the power.

I didn't respond. I just stood there.

"Did you buy a chair on your shopping trip? It's really uncomfortable on this floor."

I looked at him. At the tired, terrifying man and I felt... pity. Wait, no. Fear? I don't know. I really don't know.

So I got the chair.

I walked inside, picked up the chair I bought, and handed it to Eli. The ridiculous man who came from the box.

"Thanks. You're a good person aren't you, what's your name?"

"It's Olivia."

"It's nice to meet you Olivia, why don't you take a seat?"

He gestured to the floor of the shed. The one that I'd painstakingly put together with my own hands just the day before. My shed. It infuriated me. How could he just move into my life and treat me like the guest?

It made me angry, but I obeyed him regardless, he was hypnotic. There was something special about Eli. So I sat cross legged on the ground as he loomed over me on the chair.

I felt so small.

"I've been hoping that a good person would buy my box for such a long time. I'm so glad it was a good person like you. I think we're going to get along great Olivia, don't you?"

I crossed my arms and turned my head. I felt so uncomfortable. He spoke about his presence in my space like it would be long term, like he was intending to stay. I fought all my fear and all my anger—*I'd gotten good at that*—then I spoke.

"Eli, it's been a pleasure, but you need to leave, this is my home. I'm not intending to share it. I'm sorry."

His eyes narrowed.

"You paid for me, though. That's a contract. No taker backers. This is *my* home, you're merely a custodian. Don't you want us to have a good relationship, Olivia? The ball's in your court."

I shook. I tried to conceal it, but I think he saw. It's like he could smell my fear. He knew I was alone, vulnerable. It was like he knew there was no one I could call to help me.

"I... I'm sorry." I stuttered. "You need to leave."

I was firm. I tried to be. It took everything I had to muster up the courage to say those words. *I'd done it before,* I thought, remembering the last time I removed a man from my life, *I can do it again.*

The moment my words were finished it kicked in. The pain. He smiled a twisted grin as I felt my insides dance, writing into all the wrong positions. I'd never felt pain like it.

"I told you, Olivia, the ball's in your court. Are you sure you won't let me stay a while?"

I clutched my stomach. I wanted so desperately to penetrate my own torso and manually place my own organs back into the correct position, but the pain wouldn't let me. It wouldn't even let me move.

"You can stay." I spat through gritted, grimacing teeth.

The pain stopped in an instant. Eli stood up from the chair and outstretched a hand as I collapsed to the ground. He looked shinier somehow, not quite as tired as before. More handsome than he had been.

"Shucks, you've made the right choice, Liv. We're gonna be great. I can tell."

I sat on the floor, winded for a few moments before I finally took his hand. I wasn't sure if it was fear or fascination that made me take it. I don't know if I was just weak or if something was truly wrong with me. Nevertheless, I took his hand.

"I'll help you with the painting. We can do this place up real nice, I'm so excited to start a life with you."

My stomach churned. He was being so nice, it seemed so genuine. But how could a man be flat packed? And how could he cause *so much pain* just looking at me?

I'm ashamed. I'm ashamed of how well I assimilated. I accepted my fate. That night I bought Eli dinner, a chicken casserole, and he gently suggested that next time I bought a curry.

It sounds small, just a dinner request, but it wasn't. He shot me that twisted smile, and I obeyed.

The next day I bought curry. I questioned myself at every moment. Why was I doing as I was told? Why was I obeying a man that claimed he came in a flat pack box? Why didn't I just lock it, let him rot? Or better—*why didn't I just burn it?*

I wish I could answer those questions. I wish I had a simple answer, but I didn't. Maybe I was scared. I was, I really was.

Maybe I thought I deserved it. I was weak, right?

Or maybe I needed the validation he gave me when I handed him the curry and he told me what a good person I was. That's sick, right? That I'd let someone infect my entire life for a few brief moments of gratitude.

Life with Eli became routine.

I went to work, I shopped. I cooked for us, I cleaned for us. I spent every day and every evening in the shed. With him. Then at night, I went back to the house, I shut myself in and I cried.

I cried for my freedom, for the pain I was in, for the desperation of my situation, and for the lack of willpower in me. I didn't fight. I just cried.

It went on like that for a while. A long time, in fact. Just a routine. A mundane routine.

Things were good. Or as good as they can be when a man like that lives in your shed. He helped me with the DIY, kept me company and he kept me focused, even if it was on my own misery.

Then one day a work colleague asked me for drinks. I didn't get invited places often; I felt a little buzz of joy that I'd been thought of. I wondered what Eli would do while he waited. Did it really matter? *He lived in a box.*

I felt free having drinks. It was liberating. I didn't have to think about how lonely I was. How lonely I wanted to be. The garden and the house and the man in the shed disappeared with every sip. For a moment I felt normal.

My peace was short lived. I had to go home, had to go back to *him*.

He was furious.

"I was hungry Olivia. I can't leave this shed, not like you can. Do you know how that feels?! To have no freedom… no power?!"

I laughed. I didn't mean to, but I did. It was ironic. I had all the freedom in the world, he was right. Yet I was chained. And he kept those invisible chains, wrapped right around the beating heart in my chest, on a tight leash in his own hands.

I was so trapped I couldn't breathe.

"Do you think that's funny? *To mock the man in the box?*" he snarled.

I stopped laughing. I felt a knot form in my stomach, like my insides were twisting. And then they *were* twisting, all out of place, wiggling around inside me like knives dancing past my flesh, leaving tiny slices wherever they scratched.

His smile twisted too. Into that sinister, wry grin that I'd feared for all these mundane, uneventful months.

I doubled over, screaming.

"Be quiet, Olivia, the neighbours will hear you. Do you want any more interference in our life?!"

Just like that he dropped the smile. *Dropped the pain.* I stopped screaming and stayed silent.

"I'm sorry, you gave me no choice. You know that, right? I can't be mocked; my dignity is all I have in this box." His words were apologetic, but there was no soul behind them. They weren't genuine.

I nodded as my own tears ran down my face, coating my lips in a salty flavour. I sniffled back snot that tried to escape my nose. I couldn't blame it; I'd try to escape too. *Why the fuck hadn't I tried to escape?*

"Do you ever want more than just this shed? More than a box?" I asked carefully, words shaking as I stumbled to my feet, dusting myself off. I was terrified to upset him. I didn't know how strong his powers were; why he had such a hold over me.

I wondered, if I was so terrible, so oppressive, then why did he stay?

"I came with the shed, Olivia, I've told you that from day one. I can't leave… I don't exist outside this shed."

"What do you mean you don't exist?"

"Exactly what I said, are you dense? If I step outside, I disappear. I'm gone. *Poof.* And so is our life together. Then it's just you, alone. Would you have any of *this* if it were just you?"

He gestured around him, around the beautifully furnished, dimly lit shed. There were fairy lights strewn around the perimeter of the roof, perfectly painted walls, a homely feel and my beautiful, expensive rug.

He was right. I couldn't have done that alone. It would never have looked as good. *He gave me that.* He helped make it the shed of my dreams, just how I wanted it.

He made it perfect, but there was no peace. There was no haven. There was just obligation, control, and pain. He gave me that too.

"Have you ever tried?" I asked.

"Why would I try to leave existence? Don't you want me here, Olivia? You did buy me."

His tone was irritated, I realised I was pushing my luck. Making him angry. I was terrified of what he might do. Could he take my organs out? Force them out of my mouth if he got mad enough? Could he do things far worse than the pain I'd already felt?

I dwelled on his words. I did buy him, but I didn't know what I was getting. Did that make it my fault? Maybe.

"You're right. I'm sorry Eli, of course I want you here."

I hobbled to my kitchen, I made food and I sat with him. He smiled sweetly; he didn't look half as tattered as he had when we first met anymore. He was strong, fit, handsome. I did that. Maybe that was what it was all for. Maybe I was making him better.

I bid the man in the shed goodnight and I cried myself to sleep again.

How did my life take the turn that it did? *Why me?*

I laid in bed and thought about what he'd said. He wouldn't exist if he left the shed. Did he mean that? He came in the box. It took me a long time to accept that.

Maybe he just couldn't see beyond the four walls that trapped him, or beyond the miserable life we shared.

Maybe he'd be happier if he could just leave the shed. *I hated him.* He terrified me. And I just wanted to make him happy.

A thousand options ran through my mind. If I tried to free him would he hurt me? I could try to run, but where would I run to? How would I cope on my own? I'd never done that. Been alone.

I left one man. Made my own home, bought my own shed, and it came with another man. What would I do without him? What was Olivia all about?

It terrified me. The idea that I couldn't exist without Eli. But that was just the hold he had on me. He couldn't leave the shed and I couldn't leave him. So I just left it.

Months more passed. Months of feeding him, pandering to him, listening to his every story. He exhausted me. As I got weaker, he got stronger. I stitched up every tear in his suit, glued the holes in his shoes... I fixed him.

At the expense of me.

The fear I felt daily chipped away, it robbed my sleep, my looks and my sanity.

The final straw came when I told him I was tired and wanted to go to bed early one night. He said that I didn't care about him and that he wished someone else had bought his box.

"You took me on Olivia, you chose that and now look at you! You can't even keep your eyes open for our last hour together this evening. How could you be so selfish? You know you're all I have."

I apologised, I pleaded, I retracted my request. It didn't matter. One more stray yawn and the twisted smile was back, the sinister tone that laced every word he spoke was thrust to the forefront of his vernacular. He spoke with bile, venom.

I snapped. Wait. No. My wrist snapped. Fuck. The bone inside it let out an almighty crunch, and I fell to the ground in agony.

My organs did that familiar dance. I writhed and convulsed, contorting into shapes that only caused more pain. It was worse this time. Every time it got fucking worse.

He just stood there and smiled. He tormented me like that for a few minutes before finally he let up.

"I suppose I'll see you tomorrow then. Goodnight Olivia, sleep well."

I hobbled from the shed to the house, my arm swelling steadily beneath my shirt.

Why was I doing this to myself? Why the fuck was I letting him do this to me?

I snapped.

Not my arm this time, but me. I couldn't live like it anymore. Live in terror of his constant attacks. He would lull me into a false sense of security and then strike. My guard was never down anymore, I was just a ball of anxiety.

I put on my pyjamas, got into bed and for the first time since Eli had arrived in my life I didn't cry. Instead, I waited until it was pitch black outside and I was certain that every neighbour's lights were off.

I opened the backdoor carefully, making sure I didn't make a sound. I opened the gate at the side of the house, I had to be sure it looked like strangers.

Then I walked across the grass and set the shed on fire.

I felt sick, my hands were clammy and my wrist throbbed, the swelling from the injury growing by the second. I was a tired mess, but I didn't care. Soon I would be free. I watched as the embers turned to violent, vicious flames.

Then I watched through the tiny window in the door as he burned.

He looked back at me. He knew. He knew what I'd done and that twisted smile never once left his face, even as his face melted into nothingness.

As the shed disappeared into ash so did he. Finally, the flames ripped through enough wood for the structure to collapse and as he promised, without the shed he didn't exist.

The firemen came. I filed a report. They promised to search for the non-existent vandals that had twisted my arm as I confronted them.

Life went on.

It went on without him. I was still there, still me. But I was empty. Was this what freedom felt like? Boring. Quiet. Lonely.

Did Eli still have some sort of hold over me? Was he controlling me even in death?

It's been so very quiet for weeks now and I should be grateful. I should be pleased that he isn't there to scare me into submission and that no one's hurting me anymore.

But I miss him.

I miss the dinners, the help, the company. Even if the good was few and far between surely it had to be better than *nothing*.

I tried a few things to make myself feel better. I did some yoga, I got one of those adult colouring books and I even tried walking along a nearby coast. None of it worked, so last week I resorted to retail therapy.

Today my new flat pack arrived, complete with my brand-new shed. Tomorrow I'll build it, but until then it sits in the corner of the room, striking fear and excitement into my heart.

Feeling scared has to be better than feeling nothing, doesn't it?

I just hope the man in this box is nicer.

ANGELI

The following text is comprised of passages copied from the journal of test Subject L. Subject L was given one dose of Angeli each week for six weeks.

Day One

I took the first pill today. Dr. Jenkins took me to a room that looks kind of like my one back at home. If I'm honest I find that a little creepy. Can I write that here? Anyway, I took the pill and 2 hours in I feel fine. There's no notable difference and my perception of everything remains as it was. Nothing further to report.

Day Two

Wow. She arrived last night. I thought at first she was a trick, or an actress sent in by the doctor but she's almost translucent; she's like a hologram and it would take some seriously impressive tech to fake that. Although with the amount they're paying me to test this shit I'm sure they could afford it.

She said her name is Eloise and she lives in the same town as me. Well, it's not really my town, is it? Doc said that this pill would make me see people from another dimension, but I don't really know what I expected. She's pretty. She likes football and she sits at the end of my bed all day.

I like Eloise. But she doesn't seem to have anywhere else to go. She's calm, but is she stuck here? Or is she just in my head?

Day Five

I don't like Eloise anymore, and I want her removed. If she's not actually here, then I want this damn drug out of my system. I tried to say something when the food came through the hatch but whoever delivers it didn't respond. She smiles and she sits on the end of my bed, but I'm scared to go to sleep around her. The other night I woke up needing a piss and she was stood in the doorway of the en-suite, neck cricked almost 180 degrees, so her head was upside down.

She said hi and turned it back to face me. She was polite I suppose. But fuck me, is she creepy.

If you're reading this, doc, I want to talk.

Day Seven

I know you put the second dose in my food. I know it.

I know you put it in my food because today Robbie showed up. You didn't tell me they wouldn't be all... human. Robbie has a face like a person, but when he opens his mouth those damn pincers come out. I thought it was a bit insect-like until I saw him licking a roach off the wall. I'm scared doc, please just talk to me. Eloise is still here, and this room is becoming a little crowded. I'm writing this in the shower just to be away from them.

They're whispering.

Day Nine

I know you hear me screaming. I know whoever the fucker is that drops off my food has heard me begging you to let me out. I may not understand all the jargon in my contract but there has to be a get-out clause, right? Surely that's a thing.

Robbie and Eloise don't talk to me anymore. They talk to each other a lot though. They've developed a language I don't understand, and they seem to enjoy my discomfort. I spend all my time in the bathroom now. It's cold here.

Please, Dr. Jenkins, I know there's some humanity in there.

Day Fourteen

I don't know how much longer I can go without food. I tried to avoid everything they gave me in some convoluted hope that they wouldn't let me die in here. That hope is gone. If Dr. Jenkins is even real, he's enjoying my suffering. If you're reading this, I don't know who you are but please dear god, help me. Robbie and Eloise are unbearable. They don't hurt me, but I live in constant fear. I want to go home.

Day Twenty

I don't know why I'm still writing this damn journal. I just hope that someday someone will know what these fuckers did to me.

With the arrival of Rock a few days ago shit's gotten crazy in here. Rock doesn't like Robbie, but he really likes Eloise. He doesn't seem to recognise my presence at all. I don't know if he can't see me or if I'm just insignificant.

Eloise tried to talk to me for the first time in weeks last night. She said, "the worst is yet to come." I damn near pissed myself all over the floor. I'm contemplating topping myself… anything has to be better than this.

Day Twenty-Three

They're all dead. Rock. Eloise. Robbie. *She ate them all.*

Day Twenty-Nine

I don't know how I'm still alive. Even though she was translucent, I can still smell Eloise rotting on the floor. I thought someone would've picked what's left of them up by now. She didn't seem to want to eat the heads.

What is she, doc? What is she? And why isn't she trying to kill me? She knows I'm there; she's not like Rock, she makes eye contact. But she never says a word. She took them out quickly and she guards the door as the food comes in. I wonder… if she's trying to protect me.

I don't feel as unsafe with her as I did the others.

Day Thirty

He doesn't talk either. But I like him. I haven't given them names; what they are doesn't need a name. They like me too. They're going to free me.

Day Thirty-Four

We will come for you. We will come for you. We will come for you. We will come for you. We will come for you. We will come for you. We will come for you. We will come for you. We will come for you. We will come for you. We will come for you. We will come for you. We will come for you. We will come for you. We will come for you. We will come for you. We will come for you.

This was the last journal entry made by Subject L. On day thirty-five unknown forces compelled Dr. Arnold Jenkins to open the contained room and check on the subject, an action the foundation had strictly prohibited. Dr. Jenkins was found alone in the room, missing his eyes and liver. There was no sign of the heads of the three individuals mentioned in the journal, although clean-up crew did mention a deathly stench that didn't match the freshness of the doctor's corpse.

We continue to search for Subject L and in the meantime, we are submitting these transcripts to the board to request we cease production of Angeli immediately.

THE REGULARS

I'm a 19-year-old girl and I work as a waitress at a small local restaurant in the town I'm currently at university studying in. The job is supposed to help me gain some work ethic and, more importantly, money while I'm away from home.

Anyone who's worked in the service industry knows how it can be. Much longer hours than you're contracted, being called in at the last minute, awful customers and even worse managers. It wasn't always bad, but it certainly wasn't often good. I hated the job itself, but without it I could barely afford to eat, let alone go out and socialise. The people I worked with made it bearable.

Work became my social life.

I missed home a lot. I grew up in a beautiful home with a wonderful family. My mum and dad were so perfect they were like catalogue parents. They both worked in medicine, my dad as a doctor and my mum as a surgeon. They were both fit, healthy, and loving.

My little sister was 16 and looked different to me. She had olive skin and darker hair that flowed down her back, while my unruly blonde curls stopped at my shoulders. People were often surprised we were sisters, but once we interacted you could tell we were related. No one had ever seen sisters so close. We were friends. Most siblings I knew fought constantly. But not me and my sister, we were blessed with a great relationship.

I guess all the privilege I'd grown up with had hit me when I arrived at uni. I made friends with so many people from diverse backgrounds and realised just how blind to the world I was. I'd sailed there while others had almost worked themselves to death just to get a chance. Seeing how easy I had it in comparison made me feel like an entitled brat.

I got the waiting job to try to learn to function on my own. I even called my parents and told them to stop sending me money. I was determined to be independent. My friend Kesi worked there, and it was nice to work with a friend. We could rant about rough shifts and shitty customers together.

Me and Kesi mostly worked the night shift. We would start at 5pm and the restaurant closed at around 11pm, depending on how many customers decided to stick around after the official 10.30 close. We would stay to mop the floors and clean down the seating area.

We got tons of abuse on the night shift. People tend to get more drunk during the dinner rush and love to take it out on their waitress. Don't get me wrong, not all customers are assholes, but the assholes stand out.

It was worth it for the generous drunk tips though.

Kesi got it worse than me, due to her Tanzanian heritage. She had one regular customer that made the same awful slave joke as she delivered his food every time. The manager never did a damn thing, and the owners were never around. The guy left a huge tip but was a blazing racist who made her cringe every time she saw him in her section.

We'd gotten used to it. After I had a guy ask if my private parts were on the menu in front of his children I didn't think it would be possible to feel too uncomfortable with a customer again, I was desensitised.

Then around 4-5 months ago that changed. A man was seated in my section. He was dining alone, and I always try to make some effort to make single diners feel special. They're often sweet and seem to never really cause a fuss.

I walked up to his table ready to take his drinks order. I could feel him staring at me all the way across the small restaurant as I approached his table. He was middle aged, probably around the same age as my parents. He looked dishevelled with his hair a little tufty and unkempt, he wore a pair of glasses that were slightly wonky and had stains on his tattered jacket. And he didn't once break his stare. His eyes were on me the entire time.

The closer I got the more uncomfortable it made me feel. He didn't look happy, yet at the same time he did. He just kept staring, with this strange expression on his face, he looked at me like I was some sort of deity in the flesh.

I asked him what he would like, remaining friendly and professional, but decided not to interact too heavily. Something about this guy gave me the creeps.

He ordered a bottle of dry white wine and I knew I was in this for the long haul. I delivered his bottle and poured out the first glass as he continued to stare at me with the same strange expression. In normal circumstances in the real world, I would have asked what his problem was. But this was work, he was relatively quiet, and I needed a good tip to pay for a festival ticket.

I took his starter order and walked away to serve my other tables. Every customer I interacted with blended into one, the only thing I really noticed all night was that this guy was staring at me. The entire time.

As I delivered his food, he ate, I waited other tables and walked the floor doing my job. I found myself venturing into the kitchen to escape his gaze.

The chefs laughed at me, they said that I'd just found myself a new boyfriend. The more freaked out I got the funnier they found it. But something about it made me shudder. I didn't find it funny at all.

He stayed for an hour and a half, got three courses and drank two bottles of wine. He left a decent tip. Even as he left, he watched me. He had to practically walk backwards to avoid breaking eye contact.

After closing, all I could think about was the man. It had been busy all night, and I hadn't caught Kesi until the end.

She hadn't noticed him. Damn, I was hoping someone else had, to stop me feeling so stupid.

Over the next week, I didn't think much of it. Through uni work, other customers and various events through the week, the guy who stared at me became just another weird customer. A story to be told during the after close cigarette at work.

That was until exactly a week later when the man was yet again sat in my section. This time, he wasn't alone. He'd bought a woman with him. She had curly hair that was unkempt just like his, huge bags under her eyes and a tired expression. I noticed them before they noticed me, I was glad that he wasn't alone this time. I initially thought that the woman being there might preoccupy him and stop him staring.

I was wrong.

As I bounded up to their table after a deep breath my heart sunk. The woman caught sight of me and looked at me in shock and horror. She pulled the same strange expression that the man had pulled the first time and was pulling again. They stared at me in perfect unison.

I took their drinks orders and rushed off, hearing inaudible whispering as I walked away. Something was not right. Kesi was working this time and had the section closest to mine this time. I caught her in the kitchen and told her that he was back, and that the lady was doing the same thing.

Sure enough, the behaviour continued. As I took their food orders after delivering drinks, the woman tried to speak to me.

"Chloe..." she began softly. But the man grabbed her knee, not breaking eye contact with me.

I wondered how she knew my name, but of course during my initial scripted waitress greeting I tell them my name. Not many customers remember it though and the restaurant was fairly high end, so we don't wear name badges. They were really paying attention. It made me edgy.

The man proceeded to interrupt her with his order, ordering for her as well. I never like when people order for their partner, it seems a little archaic. I didn't stick around, but the whispers seemed more pointed this time.

They stayed for two hours this time. The man continued to stare at me as he had the week before and the woman zig zagged between staring at me in the same fashion and presumably "powdering her nose" in the lady's room. She came back twitchier each time and it would've accounted for the bags under her eyes.

Again, they left a generous tip, but it did nothing to subside the feeling of deep unease.

At close Kesi told me she'd noticed it too. She said it had been creepy the way they'd looked at me. It may sound like a huge overreaction, but neither of them took eyes off me unless I removed myself from their vision. It was nice to know someone had seen it.

They returned the next week.

And the next.

And the one after that.

I tried to swap shifts, but I couldn't do it around my uni work, and I tried to swap sections. One of the nights Kesi served their table for me and even as they told her their drinks orders they watched me. It was like no one else in the room was present to them.

I had complained to the manager, but he just laughed it off. He couldn't speak to customers about simply looking at one of his staff members, as he put it.

After a few weeks, the guy started making more lone visits at random times of the week. He would come for drinks and something small to eat. If I weren't on shift, he wouldn't stay long. The manager would even joke to me when I came to work that my boyfriend had been in and run home because I wasn't there. The chefs found it hilarious.

No one realised how much it frightened me.

They started showing up everywhere, just shopping in the same stores as me, walking past me in the street, taking the same buses I did to different stops each time. I only ever saw them for a flash, or it was too crowded for me to stop them and ask them why they were following me.

One night recently I could have sworn I saw the woman. Staring into my window from across the road on campus. As I picked up my phone to call the police and looked up, she was gone. I sobbed that night, conflicted between genuine terror and the concern that I was reading so deeply into nothing.

After seeing the woman out of the window, I started carrying a rape alarm. I just wanted something loud enough in case I was ever grabbed. This couple seemed so fixated on me that I felt vulnerable all the time. I didn't know whether or not to call the police. I had no real evidence, and they hadn't done anything wrong. Can someone be arrested for making you uncomfortable?

Every week I dreaded that shift. The one I knew they'd be there for. My rape alarm didn't make me feel much safer. The tip was no longer worth it. I was losing my sanity over this.

This weekend just gone I was dreading it more than ever. I had seen them a grand total of 12 times throughout the week, and who knows how many times they were watching without me knowing. That same sad but happy expression that they pull every time.

I don't know what came over me. Maybe it was the lack of sleep, maybe it was the sleeping pills I'd been taking to help with it. More than likely, it was the fact that Kesi was away for the weekend and I didn't have a lift home that night. Whatever it was, something convinced me to pack a knife in my purse that night.

Despite what happened, I'm still glad I did.

As expected, the couple came for their weekly booking. I didn't serve them, the best I could get out of the manger was to at least serve them himself so that I didn't have to.

They stared at me the entire time, as they always do. The lady kept pulling something out of her pocket and looking at it under the table. The man occasionally broke his gaze to look at whatever she had in her hands and the back at me. It seemed to surprise him every time.

Their food came and went, and they left, the woman rustling something in her pocket as they walked out the building. They walked straight past me and I only caught four words from the man to the woman as they left.

"Not yet, but tonight."

It sent shivers down my spine. There was no one here that could take me home. All the other closers stayed much later than I did for kitchen and cashing up and I knew when I left, I was on my own. I knew they were going to do something to me. I was so glad I'd packed that knife, even if this whole situation was making me feel paranoid, at least I had some protection.

I finished my close, and as the time rolled around to leave, I could feel my hands shaking and my palms sweating as I made my way down the road towards the bus stop.

Every shadow made me twitch; it was quiet out. The shops were all closed and there weren't many people around, just the occasional car going past.

I could feel footsteps behind me, and I knew they were following. I kept a hand inside my bag, ready to grab hold of the knife if I needed. When I sat down at the bus stop, I finally saw the outlines of two figures approaching me.

I wasn't going to give them any time to harm me. I ran as fast as I could, they kept up well considering their ages and respectively tired faces. I thought they were going to catch me until I darted across the road.

The last thing I heard was the lady scream the name *Harley*. Then there was a large bang and the whole sound around me went numb. That doesn't make much sense, but I don't know how else to explain it, everything had this dull muffled feeling to it. Like the world was going in slow motion.

I turned around to see the mangled bodies of my stalkers, laid out in front of the bus that had abruptly broken after hitting them.

Bones were jutting out of bloodied rips in their flesh. The expression hadn't left their eyes though, and somehow it still looked like they were staring at me.

I ran towards the wreckage, ran to the couple to check for pulses as the horrified bus driver got out of his vehicle. As I checked the woman over, I felt a crunching in her pocket and quickly grabbed the contents—two folded up, wrinkled bits of paper—and without looking at them shoved them in my bag while I continued to give futile CPR.

The couple were dead.

I gave my statement to the police, told the paramedics what had happened and tried to explain to the bus driver that I was being followed and it hadn't been his fault, they literally ran out in front of him. It seemed like hours before they finally let me go home.

As I collapsed into my bed, I remembered the pieces of paper that I'd stuffed in my bag and got them out. I unfolded and smoothed them out and gasped at the contents.

One was an article from 20 years ago, in a national newspaper. The headline read.

We named her Harley. The story of the couple whose baby was stolen from the womb.

The photo showed the couple holding baby girls' clothes and looking devastated. The article explained that the woman had spent a lot of time recovering in hospital from the forced c section at 8 months. She was only alive due to the evident surgical knowledge of the unknown attackers who had broken into their home and performed it while her husband worked away.

The second piece of paper confirmed my worst fears. It was a printed photograph of what appeared to be the lady's mother. With unruly blonde curls to her shoulders, and the face a mirror image of mine.

This morning the newspapers reported the identities of the victims and mentioned their past tragedies.

My parents keep calling to see how I'm doing after the incident. I thought I was scared of the couple, but that was nothing compared to how terrified I am now every time that phone rings.

I HATE BEING PICKED LAST

I'm not sure what it is. What exactly has always been wrong with me? Some people are just magnetic, they draw in everyone around them but not me.

It's like I'm the other end of that same magnet, repulsing all those who come near me. It wasn't pointed. It wasn't an outward disdain; I've just always been practically invisible.

A middle child, I played second fiddle to my rebellious older sister and my disabled younger brother. My parents didn't have enough time for me. Enough love.

I didn't have any friends at school. Not one. I was lonelier than the other loners. More invisible. More alone.

Sports classes were the worst. I'd stand in a line, filling the empty space I'm sure they saw and wait patiently for my name. Desperately seeking the approval of my peers I'd anxiously rock on my toes; maybe my movement would help them notice me?

It never came.

"Danny, I guess you're with the first group."

The teachers always tried to be enthusiastic. Futile attempts to make it somehow less obvious that I'd been rejected by everyone around me. I suppose I was grateful for it, at least for that brief moment that they pitied me I was seen.

It followed me into adulthood. That *repulsion*—the atmosphere around me that made me invisible. I did well in school. I suppose it wasn't much of an achievement when you consider the lack of distraction. My academic achievements took me far, but they never gave me a social life.

When I entered the world of work, I hoped things would change. I hoped that I could reinvent myself and be a different shade of invisible. A more visible one, maybe.

Just one friend would've changed my life; an interaction with the opposite sex or an invite to an office party would've done.

I tried. I really fucking tried. I made conversation, showed interest in the group and even tried to host a gathering at my flat but none of it worked. After an entire year the woman who sat at the desk opposite me asked my name.

I went through so many options in my mind. I could kill myself; Wade into the ocean and be swept away with the waves, feeling the misery in me replaced with an artificial, oxygen deprived euphoria.

Or maybe I could go out with a bang? Force the world to notice me in a blaze of glory. Load up a bag, drive to the office and blow the brains out of every single person in there. Boom. Maybe then they'd notice me.

I sound nuts now. I know. Honestly, that's not me. But how many of you can say it's never crossed your mind? That you've never felt that angry, or alone or just plain empty?

Yeah. You have haven't you.

So, I tried to be better. I started listening to podcasts, reading self-help books and spending every second of spare time trying to be the best version of myself. A version that I didn't hate. A version that others would see. A version that didn't want to die anymore.

It took a while. I repeated the words "I'm worth it" what felt like a million times. I didn't believe any of it at first, but if you tell yourself something for long enough, then eventually you'll start to believe it. Especially if it's something you desperately want to be true.

They call it positive affirmation.

That's what Jonathan called it, anyway. He was a charismatic man. One of those magnetic people that I'd spent my life so jealous of. A self-help guru. Everyone in a mile radius noticed Jonathan. He had an online following so devoted they bordered on frightening.

I don't know if I was attracted to Jonathan as a person, I think really it was about what he had. All those qualities I wished I possessed that just oozed from every hair on his flawless, quaffed do.

Either way, I paid the money. His events weren't cheap. Promises like the ones he made never are. What's a few thousand for spiritual awakening? For the chance to transform your life and ascend to a superior plane of existence.

I ate that shit up. I would. I'm the prey that those people hunt, one of the people that turn into pound signs when they enter that magnetic force field. The field the privileged possess. I paid. Even the extra thousand it cost to meet him before the event, desperate to absorb some of that energy.

The event was intimate for such a popular speaker. Only fifty or so of Jonathan's most dedicated supporters. It was the end of a long tour that he'd promised would be so much more than the others. Most had followed him around the whole country.

They all mingled in a lobby with hot drinks and scrawled name tags. I tried to join the groups but I was left awkward, standing a little too close to circles I wasn't welcome in. I met the man himself only minutes before he gave his talk; the one that promised to change us forever.

His green eyes were mesmerising, I wasn't sure anyone had looked me in the eye like that before. I felt like he saw me. He really *saw* me. I felt a belonging that was so foreign. Our interaction was only a brief greeting but even still I walked into that lecture hall feeling different.

Ready to change.

The speech was filled with motivational drivel. The kind you find on a poorly constructed Facebook meme that your aunt sent, or on a plaque in a cheap home decor shop. It wasn't lift changing, it wasn't spiritual. But something about Jonathan was.

The group listened intently; Jonathan played on our anxieties, our fears, and our shared feeling of being an outsider. He called each person by name, made them active participants in the event.

Each person but me.

He'd forgotten me. He hadn't *seen* me at all. I was stupid to think that anyone would. Even my name tag, my personal meeting, and all my fucking cash wasn't enough. I felt the anger bubbling, but I suppressed it. Just like I always did.

I sat, seething as the crap that Jonathan spewed lost all its sparkle. I watched as the other desperate people hung on his every word and I withstood the hours of trust exercises, scenarios and role plays, all of which I was passed up for.

Then he said it.

"We've reached the end of our journey together today, to bring together everything we've learned I'm going to call each of you forward to partake in a special tea. Brewed in the Himalayas it's said to have very light psychedelic properties, it'll help you reach those spiritual heights you're yearning for."

I knew what was coming. I felt my stomach churn as I imagined the other people that had found themselves in my exact spot throughout history. I saw through the facade, through Jonathan's sinister grin, and through the brown liquid that he ladled into small plastic cups. I knew, but I did nothing. What was the point? They were all so entranced. Who would listen?

After each cup, he called a name.

"Denise."

"Jared."

"Barbara."

"Natalia."

He called name after name as I sat in the back row and waited. I waited for the commiseration. For the final cup filled with dregs to be placed in my hand, a perfect metaphor for the teacher placing me in a sports team. The leftover.

It never came.

I looked around me as every person in the room stared intensely at Jonathan, entranced by his beautiful lies, his idyllic deception. All of them holding a small plastic cup as I scraped at my own empty hands, terrified for what would come next.

Jonathan poured the last cup. The last plastic cup, the one that was filled with the dregs. My heart skipped a beat as I waited one last time for my name. For the last time I'd be picked last.

But he didn't.

He raised the glass and smiled at the others. In perfect unison they all consumed their cups and started to mingle and laugh with those around them Jonathan made a satisfied *ahh* as he savoured the very last sip.

I shook. I scratched. I tried to think of a million things to do, but I couldn't. Maybe I was wrong. Maybe I was just bitter that I hadn't been picked.

But I wasn't wrong.

I noticed Jonathan first. Of course I did. The blood that dripped from the corners of his eyes, his ears, his nose. The smile that never left his face even as he dropped to the ground. I turned and watched them bleed around me. I searched for someone else. Another invisible. Maybe I just hadn't noticed them.

But I was alone. In minutes they were dead, a sea of bloodied corpses and me, a space where one more should be.

Is it bad that I still wish I'd been picked first?

I'M ONE OF FOUR SISTERS AND WE WERE ALL BORN CURSED

The odds of having a set of identical quadruplets are somewhere between one in eleven and one in fourteen million. The probability of a birth like that occurring during a lunar eclipse is even less, but my sisters and I have defied odds since conception.

We never got to meet our mother, she died giving birth to us. We've seen photos of course, of a face similar to each of our own, yet unfamiliar all the same. She left a hole in our lives that had never and couldn't ever be filled by anyone.

Our father struggled. He lost the love of his life and was faced with four identical copies of her that needed every waking moment of his attention. It was too much for anyone to take, and thwarted any real love he had to give. I don't remember a time that our father could bear to look at any of us.

Perhaps that's why our individual afflictions went unnoticed for so long. Or perhaps he noticed them from the start, and it was why he chose to be so distant. Maybe he considered us monsters.

It isn't much use to dwell on it now, the damage was done the moment our mother took her final breath, and her fourth baby took her first. It was just the way things were.

We were raised by a string of nannies, each less equipped to deal with us than the last. The cold, loveless childhood we endured only strengthened our bond as sisters.

I don't know what caused it, some phenomena have no worldly explanation, but each of us were born with our own unique ability. When we were young they felt like superpowers, but as we got older it became clear that we hadn't been given gifts at all, rather curses that we were resigned to live with.

That's why I'm writing this. I want to end my curse; I don't want to continue living this way.

***

Maribel was the oldest, four minutes ahead of Amelia. It was her particular scourge that alerted our first nanny to just how unusual we were. As babies, it was less obvious, but Maribel's power was unavoidable.

My oldest sister was able to visit anywhere in the world at a moment's notice, using nothing but her mind.

She would do this in her sleep, leaving a trace of herself behind to keep her grounded to home. Maribel would still be visible in her bed, but if you reached out to touch her your hand would travel straight through. She only ever left behind just enough to tether her to reality.

It frightened the first nanny; she was terrified to drop the tiny baby if she suddenly went travelling and became an apparition of a child. My sister would always wake giggling, having returned from her adventure.

As we grew and our communication skills developed, Maribel began to describe her journeys. By the age of five she could name streets surrounding the Eiffel Tower without ever having read about it, described bright and vivid green rainforests along with expanses of ice as far as the eye could see.

I'm not ashamed to admit that I was jealous of Maribel's ability. Who wouldn't be, right? Her life was an endless holiday.

It seemed so much fun and I was the latest to bloom of my sisters, so while she was wandering deserts, I was left to believe that I was the only *average* sibling.

Eventually, she brought things back. Objects and artefacts from places that she visited in her dreams. At first a stone from the Great Wall of China, then the shed skin of a deadly Australian snake, a Moroccan lantern and the most beautiful flower I had ever seen, that she claimed came from the Himalayan region.

Every time she would return with a souvenir she would sleep for an incredibly long time, sometimes entire days depending on the size of the gift, it really took it out of her.

Our father home-schooled us… well he hired a tutor to do so. As a result, we spent the entirety of our childhood in one home, with only each other and the hired caretakers for company.

He was reluctant to expose us and our talents to the general population. In retrospect I suppose it was for the best, but at that time in our lives we couldn't have anticipated the problems we were going to face. His decision to deprive us of a real childhood simply seemed cruel.

I remember us learning geography at about 8 years old in the living room and I was growing thoroughly tired of Maribel's incredible knowledge. She could rattle off capitals and continents as if it were nothing.

The teacher quit when Maribel perfectly described her Colombian hometown, and her family living there. As a catholic, she thought we were the work of the devil. It was offensive, sure, but it didn't stop my sister from acing every test.

If I were capable, I'm sure I would've been quite annoyed, but with the exception of Amelia we are all incredibly calm and non-confrontational. It felt like Maribel was cheating, and more poignantly, that she had a chance that the rest of us didn't to escape our prison.

My jealousy didn't stop me from loving her. Of all of us, Maribel was the dreamer. Her intense wanderlust and whimsy were part of what made her so beautiful. She sported a sun kissed tan or cold, flushed rosy cheeks at any given time and the joy at what she'd seen was always present in her eyes. She loved us, too. I can't count the amount of time we ate French patisserie for breakfast in the small room we all shared.

When we reached twelve Maribel's ability had grown much stronger, we were used to her sometimes spending days away, with nothing but the holographic version left. She had started to daydream; and was able to visit the places that her mind created.

I remember her giving me a tiara once. It was the most stunning thing I've ever laid eyes on. Maribel had slept for two days after a journey, but when she woke she feebly handed it to me.

"I want you to have this Edith, I dreamed it just for you."

It was made up of an otherworldly material, it resembled the precious metals that would make a real one but felt like liquid in the hand and glowed a gentle blue—my favourite colour.

What looked like gems were set into various places, but as I tried to run my fingers across their surface my digits went straight through the bursts of colour, the gems more like vibrant orbs.

I still have it. As I type right now, it's sat in front of me as a reminder of my beautiful sister and the amazing things that her ability gave her. It's the only thing I have left that proves there's a beauty in our afflictions, despite the fates they doomed us to.

It was only a few days after she gave me the tiara that Maribel nightmares began. Instead of describing gorgeous natural landscapes she had started talking about places that were just infinite dark voids. Monsters that she couldn't see, that would follow her in the dark.

My father didn't take her seriously. He spent so little time with us that I doubt he understood the strength of her power. He put it down to the average nightmares of a little girl. Over the weeks, she grew more disturbed.

Travelling in her nightmares had the opposite effect of doing so in her dreams, she didn't sleep for days. Instead, she couldn't sleep for days.

My sister deteriorated so fast that none of us knew what to do. The sleep deprivation led to more nightmares, which lead to no sleep and became a vicious circle. I spent a lot of time with her, holding her hand and willing her to spend some time in Brazil, or Switzerland. Anywhere but the dark place.

As was the nature of her power, it got stronger, the nightmares got longer and eventually, she bought something back.

It happened in the middle of the night. All we heard was screaming and gasping for air that jolted the three of us awake. Maisie tried to turn on the light, but it was pointless. The tiny black creature, digging into Maribel's chest, that we could only glimpse in the millisecond before the light blew back out, absorbed it all.

My father woke to our screams and opened the door to see what was happening, but as he pushed it further, the creature absorbed any light being let in. It plunged the entire house into darkness.

I would say that I probably only saw the creature itself for a total of half a second in all the flashes. But that was enough for it to live in my memories for the rest of my life.

When the room erupted into light, the creature was gone, and so were the gasps for air. Maribel laid there, face twisted in terror, unmoving. My father didn't say a word, he just stared silently at his dead daughter.

As each of us realised it wasn't a trace she'd left behind, that it was actually our beautiful sister left on the bed not breathing the room felt heavy with emptiness. Her nightmares had followed her back and she'd died frightened and alone in the dark.

The room was more silent than it had ever been before. The pain in my stomach twisted into a numbness and I remember the complete absence of feeling. Amelia wailed.

***

Amelia wouldn't let us grieve for Maribel. I resented her for it at the time, I wanted the choice to feel sad about our sister but looking back now I don't think her ability would allow her to give anyone that choice. Maisie didn't feel it either, the grief. Instead, Amelia spent weeks locked in our room, feeling it for us all.

I can't imagine the pain she went through. Mostly because she took away my pain my whole life, she never gave me the chance to experience it, to compare my feelings to her own.

If you're familiar with the term empath, then you need to know that it doesn't nearly describe what Amelia was, but it's the closest description I can find.

The most sensitive of us all, Amelia would laugh louder, cry harder and love more than any of us as children. When Maribel couldn't sleep, Amelia barely did either. Unlike our older sister, her body wouldn't let her stay awake indefinitely and you would find her in burned out heaps, collapsed on the floor.

I know she tried really hard to take Maribel's pain away, to feel the nightmares on her behalf, but I've learned the hard way that none of our abilities can override the others. So instead, all Amelia could do was mourn on our behalf.

What kind of awful curse is that? Doomed to feel every negative emotion around you.

Even when we were very little, if we would play games and someone got hurt. It would always be Amelia that felt it. At the time we didn't realise that it was more literal than we suspected, she was too little. We thought she was sensitive. Some nannies even put it down to twin telepathy because of our multiple birth.

It was only when Maribel died that I confirmed the worst of Amelia's curse. I wish I could've felt the guilt of what I did back then, but you know what happened to that.

I was frustrated, as much as I could be. I had such a yearning to feel something… anything… that I was prepared to go to great lengths. Amelia was in our room, agonising over her deep depression, and Maisie was gone all the time.

I placed the otherworldly tiara on top of my head, if only to feel less alone, as I held the kitchen knife over my wrist in the bathroom. I didn't want to die, death terrified me. I just wanted to feel.

As the blade cut into my skin I felt the pressure, saw the blood, but there was nothing else. Amelia wailed from the bedroom, and I dropped the knife and ran to her.

She was bent over, clutching her stomach, tears rolling down her face from the weight of all of our grief. Then I noticed the few drops of blood land on the white linen bedsheet from the exact point on her body that I had cut on mine.

I backed out of the room, desperate to hold on to my guilt, but I couldn't. I spent the night on the sofa, wishing I could feel bad about what I'd done to Amelia.

The three of us that remained grew apart over the years. Maribel's death took a piece of each of us that we couldn't get back, and I remain convinced that it was the piece that held us together.

Amelia grieved viscerally in that room for a whole year before she came out. Maisie spent more time out than in, and I became something of a loner.

When we got old enough to leave our fathers house and to get our own places, we all did at the first opportunity. Amelia and Maisie both went to university, separately, but nonetheless they went.

Amelia studied social work and graduated with honours. She kept herself to herself while she was studying, frightened to grow close to anyone for fear of taking on all of their pain. Even after she escaped our loveless home she couldn't be a normal young woman.

I knew that social work was a terrible avenue for Amelia, and I knew from the few conversations I had with Maisie at the time that she agreed. There was nothing we could do, we weren't close enough for her to listen and in all honesty, I think we both knew that it was what she wanted.

It took a year to get the call. To find out that the job had killed her. To experience true pain for the first time in my life.

Just like Maribel, Amelia had succumbed to her curse. The case made the news at the time and to the public her death remains a mystery. I've never felt it pertinent to try to explain. After all, would you believe me after reading the headline?

Social worker found dead on the same night as a child on her caseload with matching injuries.

She reported the child to her superiors many times, made recommendations that he was removed from the situation. I was grateful that it was reported that way, people knew that she did everything she could. By all accounts, she really bonded with that boy, which I know will have been her downfall.

I went into shock for days. The sudden emotion was too much to bear. I couldn't remove the image of her being beaten to death by that monster, feeling every punch that he landed on that poor child. The other horrors she was subjected to.

The murderer ran, wanted for arrest for both killings. He still hadn't been found and the longer he remained hidden the larger the pit in my stomach grew. Right up until the moment I received the inevitable text from Maisie.

I'm going to find him Edith.

***

Maisie was the closest thing I had to a friend growing up, after Maribel's death. She was the toughest of us all, a tomboy with a brash attitude, and after Amelia died and she could feel for the first time, she became unstoppable.

All our lives Maisie's curse felt more benign than our two, barely older, sister's. I used to call her a homing device because Maisie could find *anything*.

It took a long time to notice what it was. As small children, we thought she was just better than the rest of us at hide and seek. Me and Maisie spent more time together than with the other two. We both thought that we were average compared to our powerful sisters.

She always knew where the keys were, or that toy that had been dropped down the back of the sofa. She could find any journal or snacks that you tried to squirrel away and once obsessively dug until she found a centuries old necklace buried in our garden that still dangles around my neck today.

That's when the nannies and our father knew for sure that she was special. The damn necklace was the reason I was left to feel more alone than ever before. Despite their abilities and my seeming lack of, I felt like the freak. Maisie was still a friend to me, but the dynamic between us changed. She made me feel so boring and drab.

The true potential of her powers came to light the first time that she caught a local missing person's case on the television.

The man was mentally ill, incredibly vulnerable and had disappeared days before the broadcast. After the news reporter finished talking, Maisie calmly got up, walked to the telephone and dialled the number provided for information.

"He's in the old bread factory, under the stairs, he's trapped under a piece of machine."

Then she hung up. No words. She didn't look at us or acknowledge what she had just done, just sat back down and went back to watching the television. I put little thought into it, until a few days later when the police found him.

They were just in time, and the man was exactly where Maisie had described. They plead for the anonymous tipper to come forward for questioning but, of course, no one ever did.

Maisie did the same thing every time she saw a case on the local news. We tried her on big profile cases many times with no luck. She could only find something that was lost somewhere familiar to her. I think she had to be able to visualise it, but I don't know for sure. Maisie never spoke much about her gift.

She found kids, grandparents, partners and even a serial rapist. It was incredible. What we had suspected to be the most benign gift of all was actually the one that was doing the most good.

After Maribel, Maisie poured herself into trying to find the creature that killed her. She grew completely fixated, not able to understand how something that causes that much damage could simply go missing.

It's why she was gone all the time. When she wasn't immediately successful, she started taking the bus to other towns and places she hadn't been trying to spark her talent. I tried to tell her it was futile, but she wouldn't listen. I knew the creature only existed in Maribel's nightmares.

It took her a long time to give up. In all honesty I don't think she ever really did, just focused her attention elsewhere for a while. When she left for university, she studied criminal law and policing.

Maisie became a detective and even in her first year was decorated for her unbelievable service. She had reunited so many, with people, stolen items or lost memories. My sister was the best in the business.

When Amelia died and I got that text I felt sick. New sensations of worry and fear washed over me. I lamented my recently deceased sister for keeping me emotionally numb so long, the shock of feeling was almost too much to take.

I protested. I didn't want Maisie to meet the same fate as Amelia, at the hands of the same monster. It wasn't officially her case, she lived miles from where Amelia had died and had never visited whilst she was alive.

Maisie didn't listen, the fixation was too strong, just like years before with the creature. Except this time the monster who had killed our sister was real, he was tangible.

I hadn't visited Amelia either in her year of social work. Of all the new emotions, the guilt was the strongest. For everything.

I tried to reach Maisie, I drove for hours, but my tracking skills weren't a patch on hers. I knew what to look for but had no idea how, and I just couldn't save her.

Maisie didn't die at the hands of Amelia's killer. It makes me wonder if her fate had already been written. If maybe, all of our fates were sealed the moment we were born.

Her death signalled the end of a manhunt for an active serial killer in the area she was searching for the abusive father. It's devastating, to think of a woman with such talent and potential, ultimately fooled and destroyed by a simplistic ruse.

In her search she came across a lone puppy, wandering a bit of woodland. She picked it up and immediately knew where to find its owner, so she circled back on herself, straight into the waiting camp of the woodland strangler.

The strangler had been using the puppy to lure women into the woods under the impression they were searching for the lost dog with him. He didn't expect Maisie, so he panicked and strayed from the signature that had made him famous.

Maisie wasn't strangled. He beat her to death in a blind rage instead, violently in the woods. Her screams alerted hikers nearby who called the police, and the killer, that was later proven to be the woodland strangler, was caught.

***

It should have bought me some comfort, to know that at least one of my sisters' killers wasn't wandering around free. But it didn't.

Instead, ever since I became the sole survivor I have been plagued with memories of death.

Three quarters of my soul are already gone and nothing solid remains.

My particular curse didn't present itself until Maribel's demise, but looking back I am almost certain that my ability was the first to have an effect, I was simply too young to remember.

I can't fathom a way to describe my curse as anything other than a symbol of death. Minutes before Maribel died, I saw exactly what would happen.

My vision was vivid, or as vivid as can be in absolute pitch black. I would've considered it a dream, an overactive imagination, but the sensations were too real.

Most alarmingly, I watched her die from the perspective of the creature who killed her, I was viciously digging at her chest, absorbing any life in her young body.

When I woke that night I prepared to alert someone, to wake Maribel and tell her what I'd dreamt, but it was too late. As I sat bolt upright in bed so did Maisie and Amelia at the sound of the screaming. Maribel died in agony minutes later.

I tried to understand what I'd seen and why I'd seen it from the viewpoint that I had. It was a cruel power, to be able to visualise a terrible event with no time to stop it happening. It was pointless, I couldn't use it for anything good like the others could with theirs.

I knew I would get the call about Amelia a few days before it happened. That's how long it took them to find her. After I imagined myself viciously beating her, and in turn the child, to death I knew in the depths of my heart that she was gone.

That vision was truly the worst experience of my life.

I tried to call her. I hoped I was wrong about my curse, that what I'd seen… before Maribel… that it was just a terrible dream. That my vision of Amelia had been the same. But the intense feeling of worry, the emotions filling my entire being proved that she wasn't coming back.

Yet again I'd predicted my sister's death.

It was me that alerted her local police that she was missing. I called them immediately and I could tell they didn't take me seriously, it took days, but I was persistent enough to get them to do a welfare check and when her workplace said she hadn't turned up, they searched her flat and found her.

Why couldn't this damn power give me time? Just enough time to even say goodbye, if I couldn't change their fate I couldn't understand why I was being robbed of a happy last memory.

Instead of a hug or a friendly word, I was left with visions of my sisters being brutally killed, being the killer in those visions only made it worse.

With Maisie it was much the same. After all we'd been through when I received that text, I couldn't bear to have another vision, another everlasting horrific memory. I chased her in my car for weeks, trying to guess where she might be hunting.

When the vision finally hit, I was asleep in my car. The beating convinced me that she'd found her target and I didn't recognise the woods. I had no idea who to call, but once I learned the truth, it saddened me that her mission was left unfinished.

It's been months since Maisie died. The man who killed Amelia still hasn't been found. I can't shake the feeling that I've failed my sisters and I'm plagued with recurring dreams of their deaths.

My life has become little more than a pocket of cruelty and depression, hauled up in my childhood bedroom with every curtain shut.

I dream of them all in turn, and every time I'm the killer.

Except for the fourth dream.

The fourth dream is the one that upsets me the most, the one that puts my place in this deceased family into perspective. It's the one where we're born.

The birth dream is every bit as vivid as the ones where my sisters leave this earth. This time, I see it from my own perspective. I see each of my sisters leaving the womb before me, the brilliant light as I open my eyes in the delivery room for the first time. Then it stops.

It stops as soon as my mother's heart does, as she takes her last breath. The dream is not me witnessing our birth, but witnessing our mother's death. And in keeping with the others, it's from the perspective of her killer.

I've realised that *I* am the curse. An angel of death that has bought nothing but misery to those around me. My visions weren't merely premonitions, they were a cause.

It's getting more and more difficult to type this out, as I try to blink away the images that follow my every thought, but it was important to me that my extraordinary sisters weren't forgotten. That the curses they bore were known.

I moved back in with our father when they announced the recent lockdown. I just wanted to be with family, even if all I had left was a man that could never look me in the eye.

For the first time in my life he's been a parent, making me food and drinks and checking on me all the time. I figured that the pain of losing all his other children had changed his outlook.

When I first saw it I didn't want to believe it, that he would poison his own daughter. But the vision was unmistakable, I vividly watched as I opened the pest poison and poured it into a glass that moments later would be presented to me by my own dad.

I knew what was in it, and I drank it anyway. I don't want anyone to suffer anymore because of my curse. I could see the guilt in my father's eyes as he handed it to me, and I wished I could take it away. I didn't want him to feel guilty, I wouldn't want me around either.

Just please, don't forget my sisters.

PLEASE DON'T LET THIS FAIL

Success, progress and achievements are funny things. They're the type of concepts that are hard to measure. Is someone successful because they're excelling in their chosen field or is it more to do with doing better than others?

Is success personal or is it a competition?

I don't really know the answer. I just know that I never felt like I really succeeded at anything. I had a good job, a loving wife, good friends and hobbies I enjoyed. By a measurable standard, my life should've been pretty damn fulfilling.

But I was never the *best* at any of it.

I made deputy manager at work. I married a beautiful woman after my childhood sweetheart left me to travel the world. I stayed friends with people from school that I never really liked because I just can't stand being alone. I went fishing every weekend, bought every bit of expensive gear and never caught a fucking thing.

It doesn't sound so fulfilling anymore, does it?

Almost There Arthur. That's what my *friends* always called me. Like it was a fond childhood nickname, except it wasn't. It got under my skin, tormented me and sparked so much I anger I almost left everything behind and just walked until I never had to hear it again.

Almost.

I don't mean to complain. I'd accepted my lot. And there're others out there who have it far worse, right? I know. I know that and that just makes it even worse. I'm not even excelling at misery. I can't even get fucking up right. Almost there. *Always almost there.*

Failure. That's a funny concept, too. Was I a failure because I didn't achieve any of my goals? Or was I successful because I came pretty darn close? I don't know. You'll learn that about me. I never have the answers, even if I feel like I'm close to them.

This morning began like every other. I sat at my desk, in my office, just adjacent in the hallway to the manager's bigger, more modern one. The receptionist informed me there was a man outside, claiming he had an appointment to see me. He'd only given the name Victor.

He wore a black three-piece suit, tailored much more professionally than the one I was wearing. I sat up in my chair in some masculine desperation to appear bigger.

Inside I felt two feet tall.

"What can I do for you Mr... *Victor?* are you interested in a contract for our office supplies?"

The man in the suit laughed. It ran through me in a way that a laugh never had before. I felt mocked, small... like I wasn't quite as good as he was.

"Victor is fine. No. I'm not here about office supplies, that's just what I told the lady at the front desk. I'm here for you Arthur."

I was taken aback.

"What do you mean you're here for me? We only sell office-"

"Supplies. I know. This isn't a work call. I'm here to provide you with an opportunity."

I felt my heart racing. Was I being headhunted by another company? Had someone *finally* recognised my talents?

"What kind of opportunity?" I asked, placing my hands in front of me on the desk, fingers interlocked, trying to look important.

"The sort of opportunity that would change your life, Arthur. How would you like a do over?" He leaned in, blue eyes intense and unblinking. He was so close I could smell the stale ash on his breath.

I laughed solemnly, thinking I understood what was happening. The receptionist had let a lunatic through. Haha. Another trick on Almost There Arthur.

"Thank you, Victor, but I don't know what you expect me to want to do over. If that's all, I have quite a bit to be getting on with."

I stood and outstretched a hand to shake his, but he just looked at it and grinned, planted firmly in his chair.

"What about walking off into the sunset with Alice? Ooh boy. Don't you wish you'd made that choice differently? I can give you back that choice."

Alice. The one that got away. How did he know about Alice? I sat back down, this time sinking into my chair.

"Good Arthur." He continued, wrestling control of the situation from me with ease.

"How do you know about Alice? And no. I don't wish I made a different choice, I love Linda." I hissed, blinking memories of my beautiful sweetheart back into the box I'd placed them in all those years ago.

"I know about Alice the same way I know you're lying. The same way I know that you considered leaving again this morning. That's why your passport is in your pocket. Don't pretend that everything's ok... I already know it isn't."

"Who... who are you?" I stammered.

"I'm Victor. And I'm here to offer you a do over. Brand new life? Well... maybe not brand new. I should make myself a little clearer, shouldn't I?"

"I have no idea what you're talking about."

"If you could go back to the age of fifteen and try your life all over again, would you?"

He grinned wildly, blue eyes remaining open and fixated. He was watching every move I made, every bead of sweat. I couldn't deny the offer was tempting. If I tried again, would I be able to catch a win?

Is life just one giant dice roll as to whether you win or lose? Or could I control it, knowing what I knew, with the experience I had. Was any of that even relevant, he didn't have the means to bend time and I knew it. No one did. That was fucking stupid. And cruel.

I stayed quiet for a few minutes, Victor getting ever closer. I tried to hold it in, but I couldn't, it was like he was a magnet drawing my words out of me. My word.

"Yes."

"EXCELLENT!" He boomed, standing and out stretching a hand just as I had before. "I just need one thing from you, Arthur... nothing major... totally inconsequential if you take the deal."

I pondered his words. I thought his offer was ridiculous, but Victor truly believed it. He meant every word. I'd been gullible before though, and I was used to being the butt of my friends' jokes. I needed proof.

"I'm not taking any deal without a guarantee. You can't possibly put me back, so what do you mean by do over?"

"Alas, Arthur, I can put you back! Let me show you! We're almost there." He winked and gestures to his still floating hand, as he said those last words and I cringed.

He knew everything. Maybe there was more to Victor than a lunatic or a practical joke.

I took his hand and felt a rush of energy coursing through my veins. My vision went blurry and the walls and cabinets of the office disappeared. Replacing it was a beach, deserted besides two people who I could barely make out from behind.

Bewildered I stepped forward expecting to bang into my desk, but it just wasn't there. I could feel Victor's hand, but I was alone on that beach, just watching the couple.

A few steps forward. They didn't notice me, they just stared lovingly into each other's eyes. As I continued to move, they became clearer. The man was me and the woman was Alice. Happy. Happy in another life where I hadn't failed.

I felt my hand go cold, and the vision dissipated. The picturesque beach was gently replaced piece by piece, my drab, grey office in its place. Victor sat in front of me, smirk across his face. Then he spoke.

"See. You could've had it all. Just a few different choices and you would have been *the man*. I can give you that. Do you want that?"

I felt tears rolling down my cheeks. Great. Now I looked as pathetic as he knew I was. I felt the crushing pain of every failure. The fear that if I turned him down I'd live to regret not accepting the strange offer. From the strange man.

I wanted so badly to try again. To win.

"It's a deal."

"Ah ah ah. Not yet, first you have to agree to your end of the bargain. That's how deals work isn't it. They aren't one sided, Arthur."

"Anything." I answered, knowing I'd sacrifice my whole life in a heartbeat for a moment on that beach. In that sun. *I'd have given him anything.*

"A life for a life, Arthur. *A wife for a wife.* When you've got my gift ready, I'll be there to take you to paradise. How does that sound?"

I swallowed a large lump in my throat. Victor's blue eyes had grown sinister, they were filled with a bloodlust and a malice unlike I'd ever seen. The more time I spent in his presence the more I became convinced he was telling the truth.

He had power over me. In a different way to everyone else in my life.

Tears still rolling, now for Linda and not Alice, I nodded. Not long after, Victor stood up and walked towards the door.

"Wait, how does this happen? How do I get my do over?"

"I just told you how. I'll see you when you're ready to start again."

He closed the creaky wooden office door and I sobbed. Everything had turned upside down. Could I kill her? Could I kill my wife? She did nothing wrong. If she heard the name Alice it wouldn't mean a thing to her, she always thought we were soulmates.

Soulmates. That's what me and Alice were. Maybe that life would've been better. Maybe I'd have been successful, been the manager... no. Fuck that. *The CEO.*

And if it were a do over then Linda wouldn't ever meet me. We wouldn't have our life and I wouldn't be miserable. She'd have another man. One more content with his lot. One that loved her like she deserved.

If Victor was speaking the truth. It would be like she never died. *Inconsequential.* That's what he said.

I sat at dinner with my wife tonight in turmoil. What if it was all true and Alice still didn't want me? What if it was never my choice in the first place? What if I just wasn't good enough to do any better at anything?

What fucking if.

I couldn't dwell on what ifs. I couldn't dwell for any longer on what could've been. It was Victor's deal or just give up entirely. Her life or mine.

So I took the selfish route.

After we'd eaten, and just before we cleared the table, I picked up a steak knife and plunged it into her chest. My hand shook and the blade went in jagged. I'd never been so frightened in my life. Do you know how hard it is to stab someone? To penetrate flesh.

What if I failed at that, too? What if I couldn't even succeed at *this?*

But I succeeded. For once in my life. I watched as the light faded from her eyes and she stared at me in confusion, wondering why someone she loved so deeply would hurt her like that.

My heart pounded. Where was he?

She laid dead on the floor and I stood, alone and covered in blood, waiting for the man in the three-piece suit.

I'd done what he asked, so where was he?

I felt the terror. I hadn't really understood terror until that moment. I was terrified it was all some kind of sick trick. Terrified I'd get caught. Terrified Linda would not get the life I'd planned for her once I got my do over.

It's been an hour and Victor still isn't here. He dangled my dream in front of me. Promised me a paradise and left me with a dead wife.

I have to try to push aside this fear, though. Maybe he's on his way.

Maybe I'm almost there.

SHE ALWAYS HELD A HAMMER

I don't remember her arrival. No pivotal moment when she walked into my life and began her reign of terror. No. She had been there as long as I could go back in my mind, and she always held a hammer.

I don't remember it, of course, but my mother always said I was a distracted baby, always gazing at something in the corner of the room. My parents probably cooed over me, wondering what an infant daydreams about.

I bet they didn't imagine *her*.

That's what I was looking at. Who I was looking at. Who I always looked at.

Why didn't anyone else see her?

She was there; on the playground at school, looming over the dinner table and watching me sleep, limp hair hanging down her back and large, clawed hammer in her veiny hands. I tried to tell as soon as I was able to. Anyone who would listen.

Imaginative kid. *Imaginary friend.* I was so easily dismissed.

They could see I was frightened; I asked my mum and dad every night to tell her to leave, and they did. They would stand in the doorway of my bedroom as if it were some kind of hollow ritual and plead with the entity to go.

They never looked in the right spot.

And she never flinched.

Her facial expression rarely changed, but I could swear that when they pretended to believe me she would look at me and smile. Smug. Knowing that I knew that their support was nothing but a lie.

And she would swing the hammer, slowly and menacingly to her side, letting her arm drop with its weight.

She never tried to touch me. Never got any closer than the corner of the room, not for a long time anyway. That didn't make sleeping any easier. How can anyone sleep with someone... *something* like that watching them.

Could you? Really?

I was a tired child.

That's why I didn't see it coming when her hammer swung down for the first time in the schoolyard and knocked my friend Jake off the swing. The swing I was pushing.

Kids fall all the time. They don't die all the time. Jake did. Jake died.

I tried to tell them all what happened, but blaming a child's death on an invisible force just didn't hack it. Especially not when the deceased child had blunt force trauma to the back of the head. I spent years in therapy, adults trying to get to the bottom of what happened.

Did you hit him with a rock?

There was no rock.

Did you push him extra hard?

There was still no rock.

All while she stood in the corner, sucking the warmth from the room, watching. Waiting.

At that age, I found it hard to understand why adults were more willing to believe that I was a murderer than the truth. It was her. Her and that fucking hammer.

I didn't get any more believable with age. Or any less tired. I tried talking to her frequently. She never once answered, just continued to look at me with the smug expression on her soulless face.

After some time, I even found her somewhat comforting. Fucked up, right? I didn't have many friends after Jake.

I didn't get any more believable with age. I just appeared more disturbed. Murderers don't get friends. They shouldn't. I shouldn't have had friends. I learned my lesson.

I was fifteen the second time the hammer came down. This time it hit far harder than it had with Jake. I wish that were only a euphemism, but I mean it literally too.

Meredith.

That was her name. My first love. My first kiss. My first. A rite of passage... destroyed. I never told Meredith about *her* and the hammer, instead I revelled in the distraction, soaking up every piece of sun that came with my beautiful love. I tried not to seem disturbed.

Meredith remained just as beautiful as she always had been. No matter how hard the hammer caved her face in as she balanced, bare skinned on top of me.

She was still beautiful. Even with her face mushed to pieces.

How can you seem *normal* after something like that? Please tell me. Suspicious childhood tragedy and then... then the untimely, violent death of an unsuspecting teenager, who had planned nothing more than losing her virginity that night.

They sent me to hospital. I never told a lie. I swear. It was her. She was always there.

She lived in my hospital room; Meredith's blood fresh on the metal claw for more time than should ever be possible. More questions, less credibility. Fifteen years old and my life was fucked.

They let me out at eighteen. No evidence. I must have seemed like every other *I'm innocent* criminal. They had everything except proof.

Pills. Injections. Therapy. Group work. They thought she went away, but she didn't. If I was crazy they would've worked, right? I just got better at pretending she wasn't there. Learned to keep my mouth shut, feign normality.

I came home.

I've spent almost a decade in this bedroom. A decade with *her*. My parents stopped telling her to leave. They stopped looking at me. They pretend they're not, but they're ashamed. Almost thirty, still home with two deaths under my belt. I wouldn't want me either.

I've considered ending it all so many times. But how am I supposed to know that it would be the end? What if she's still there, even after I die?

A decade in my bedroom. No friends. Murderers don't get friends. No love. Poor Meredith.

The only thing that kept me going was the little boy across the street. I don't know his name, he's nameless just like she is. He's full of life, more life than I've ever known. And I watch.

Nothing nefarious. Nothing *creepy*. He just reminded me of me. If *she* didn't come with me. He has friends. One that he plays with all the time just like I did with Jake. I'm jealous. No. Envious.

It's just nice to see some happiness.

His parents came to the door and shouted at mine. They didn't like me watching.

"... THAT FUCKING CREEP..."

They called me other things too. Things I don't want to write here. Things that I wondered if my parents believed. After all, they'd never believed me. I didn't stop watching. I just hid myself better.

She picked up on it eventually. The boy. The smile on my face when he distracted me from her. It was subtle. I didn't notice it at first, I was busy watching. But she noticed. She noticed everything.

She was jealous, too. Not envious.

And now I'm sitting at my window in the same bedroom I've spent the last decade in. For the first time in my life, I can breathe. I wasn't sure why at first. I was busy watching the boy. It's sunny today. It's nice.

She left.

She's never left before, but today she did. She walked out. I didn't notice. Why didn't I notice? Why wasn't I paying more attention. Murderers don't get friends. I should've remembered that.

If I'd remembered that, she wouldn't be standing a foot or so behind him. Holding her hammer.

MY SISTER LOTTIE

My sister and I got adopted at seven years old. I was so grateful; despite the fact my new parents had only adopted me because they wanted my twin, Lottie, and we couldn't be split.

I never understood why, but it was apparent that they never liked me. It was all about her. Their ignorance towards me evidenced that. As a kid it frustrated me, but it was still a step up.

Me and Lottie had been through a lot together—in the place before. We lived with big scary monsters and I was always having to protect my sister. I couldn't remember us being taken away, but I was so glad that we were.

Even though our new parents were cold and unfeeling towards me, being with Lottie made me feel secure. So I didn't mind when I wasn't allocated a bedroom, I happily slept on the floor with my sisters' spare pillow and a bedsheet with no filling.

Our parents would take my bedding away every morning when Lottie wasn't watching, tutting. They ignored my pleas to leave it.

We had a tough upbringing. Mistreatment wasn't new to me, but it was hard watching my sister flourish, while I was neglected and ignored. They bought her clothes, toys and teddies whilst I barely subsisted off scraps she bought to our bedroom after dinner.

"Shh, Dotty, I hid it in my pocket. Don't let them see." She would say as she handed me a scrunched-up piece of bread, or whatever else she could smuggle.

Lottie went to school, but I wasn't allowed. My parents never explicitly told me I couldn't go, but they never bothered to enrol me either. In fact, they avoided conversation with me altogether. Sometimes I wished they hadn't bothered to bring me home at all.

Half the time I was sure they were looking straight through me. Lottie would ask if I could come to sit with them at dinner or join them on family walks and they would just dismiss her, looking at her as if she'd made a truly wild suggestion.

I remember the first time my sister got in trouble. I don't remember what for because it was so minor. They shouted at her. They hadn't ever shouted at me before, but I didn't think they cared enough to. Is it sick that I was envious of the attention?

Lottie was shaken. We got shouted at a lot in the place before and it triggered something in her.

I had been thinking of running away for a while. I felt invisible. But that night after they shouted, my sister spent hours crying in my arms. I couldn't leave.

Lottie needed me.

I spent years on that cold wooden floor, with only an empty bedsheet for protection. My life became nothing more than ensuring hers went smoothly. I moved hazards, found lost belongings and held her hand when she cried.

Once we reached about twelve, Lottie stopped leaving me the bedsheet. She would still talk to me, but our conversations were few and far between, and there was always a doubt in her eyes. Like she was doing something she shouldn't. I was worried our parents had turned her against me.

It carried on for a long time. The cold, soulless existence I lived. All for my sister to feel secure, like there was someone on her side, always. I loved her, but I'm not afraid to admit that I was jealous of her perfect life.

It was our fifteenth birthday this week. It should've been something to celebrate, but I'd become accustomed to being less and less involved with our milestones. Lottie had her friends round for a party, and I watched from the bedroom window.

Things took a turn that night, when my parents acknowledged me properly for the first time in my life.

I thought she had forgotten about me, we hadn't spoken in a while, but when everyone was gone Lottie smuggled me a slice of cake.

"Happy birthday, Dotty."

It was the first time she'd said my name in what felt like forever. It had become apparent very early on that my parents were uncomfortable hearing it. I looked up at her and smiled, readying myself to reply when they burst through the door.

"Lottie, I thought we were past this... She's been gone a long time, you know that." My supposed mother snapped.

My heart sunk. I knew they were unfeeling, but to pretend I didn't exist was truly cruel. I tried to protest, but the words wouldn't come out. I waved my arms frantically, but none of them even flinched. I looked to Lottie for support, shouting silent words.

She used to look me in the eyes, stare right at me. We had such a connection. But it's like she couldn't hear me, or see me at all, she looked through me just like they did.

"I'm sorry, mum. I know what Dr. Truman says, I just sometimes miss her, you know." The words came out of my beautiful sisters' mouth and I wondered what she meant. A tear rolled down my cheek.

Our parents pulled her in close as she cried, and then my mother spoke words to her that tore my heart to pieces.

"Your sister was very special. She gave her life to shield you from them monsters. What they did to her doesn't bare thinking about, those type of people don't deserve children. But I'm grateful, because without them we wouldn't have you. I promise darling, we'd have loved Dotty so much."

I didn't bother to protest anymore.

Lottie hasn't spoken to me since. I think I finally understand why. I understand why I wasn't enrolled in school, or fed... or loved. I understand why I don't remember being taken away from the place before. It's because I never was.

Those monsters robbed me of my life. My parents never ignored me, we just never really met in the first place.

I've considered running away again. There has to be something more to death than this. But the more thought I put into it the more reasons I find to stay.

So here I am on the cold wooden floor, alone, sneaking a turn on Lottie's laptop while my family enjoys an outing together. It's a miserable after life but I wouldn't want it any other way.

I love my sister, and I'll always be here to protect her.

THE HOMELESS WOMAN

I'm not sure what initially drew me to her.

Maybe it was her matted, tangled grey hair. Or the fingerless gloves that I was certain hadn't always been fingerless, they vaguely resembled my own, just with more, unnecessary holes.

Or maybe it was the way she shared the crumbs of her sandwich with the pigeons on the drizzly pavement. She had nothing, but still, she wanted to share.

I didn't usually make a habit of sitting down with homeless people. I know how that sounds but it wasn't a judgement thing. I was just busy. Always rushing around.

I was busy that day, too. Yet when I saw her, I sat. I didn't care that I'd miss the train, departing from only a few metres behind where she was pitched. In fact, I was almost glad to be missing it.

Do you believe in fate? I didn't. Now I'm not so sure.

"What's your name?" The woman asked, smiling as she scattered a few more crumbs for the birds. I wondered how someone her age had ended up so down on her luck; the lines mapping her face like the rings on the wood of a tree indicated that she was at least sixty or seventy years old.

"It's Sophie." I answered, rifling in my bag and handing her a spare bottle of water I carried for the train home. She swigged it back gratefully.

"Nice to meet you, Sophie. Do you want to talk about what you're avoiding going home to?"

I was taken aback. I just saw the woman and felt compelled to sit down. I was just being a decent human being. I told her as much. She laughed.

"I'm not a charity case, although I appreciate your concern, dear. I'm free, unlike you."

"What do you mean unlike me?"

"Well? What are you avoiding going home to?"

I felt a little spooked to be honest. I didn't believe in psychics or supernatural phenomena, but the woman's insistence was difficult to ignore. And she was right, I didn't want to go home, I'd been anxious about it all day.

I just couldn't work out why.

"I don't know." I answered, taking a small piece of bread that she passed to me so I could join her feeding the birds. We sat in silence for a few moments.

"Tramp!" A young boy shouted as he rode his bike into the station and through a puddle next to where we sat. The birds flew away in a panic, and my companion was coated in filthy rainwater.

I tried to stand and confront him, but the woman grabbed my hand.

"Don't bother. He's the least of your concerns."

"Doesn't that make you angry?" I asked. The homeless woman laughed again.

"What's the point in being angry? It doesn't feel good."

Her words were simple, but they struck a chord with me. Her small talk felt poignant. Like it was supposed to mean something, a personal message. Like me sitting down on that pavement had been fate.

"Sometimes you can't help being angry."

"No." She answered, her tone less carefree than before, as she turned to face me. "Sometimes *you* can't help being angry. I can help it just fine."

"How? How do you stop that feeling?" I begged, feeling a twinge of that rotten anger, festering in the pit of my stomach. It felt spent, like it had already been unleashed and shrivelled back into its hole. I didn't know why it was there, but it always was.

"I removed the source of anger from my life."

I winced. I tried hard to rack my mind for the source of my anger. Where did that rotten little pit come from? Was it something that could be removed? Excreted like a kidney stone.

Why was I putting so much weight behind the ramblings of a woman feeding the birds on the pavement?

"There is no source of my anger."

"Yes there is Sophie. What are you avoiding going home to?"

I found myself annoyed by her question. It was the third time she'd asked it and the third time that it made that rotten little pit of anger grow.

I closed my eyes and thought of stepping off the train, making my way home, and what awaited me there. *Who awaited me there?*

"I'm avoiding my parents." I blurted, before I'd even come to terms with it myself. The woman was magnetic, forcing things out of me that I didn't know where there.

"BINGO. Took you long enough, Sophie. Has their behaviour become so normal to you that you've forgotten why they make you angry?" She laughed again, this time it was mocking, taunting me.

Just like they did.

"How do you know their behaviour makes me angry?"

The rotten little pit grew again, this time into a knot of putrid strings of emotion. Why couldn't I control it? Why wouldn't it just go away? I felt it all the time and it terrified me, the fear of wondering what it might one day make me do.

"I thought you were a little more intelligent than that. Maybe I've given you too much credit." She teased.

"Stop speaking in riddles. You sound-"

"Just like them."

She was right. She sounded like them. A perfect impression of my mother; dressing me down, telling me I'm not good enough.

On her wrinkle covered face was a carbon copy of the expression my father pulled every time he told me what a disappointment I was. I felt it hit me deep. It hurt.

The strings became sprawling vines, growing inside of me. I felt scared, desperate, but mostly angry.

"Who are you?" I begged, a tear rolling down my face.

"I thought you would've worked that out by now, too. Think about it, Sophie, really think about it. What are you avoiding going home to?"

My mind filled with little flashes. The last interaction I had with my parents just that morning, their bullying, their constant prodding, that rotten knot in my stomach that just kept growing... The knife in my hands... *The blood.*

"You already know, don't you?" I answered, my heart palpitating as I realised exactly what I was avoiding. The consequences that I'd been running from, even in my own mind.

"It's ok Sophie. You removed what made you angry from your life. I told you, I did the same."

"If you did, you're disgusting... I'm disgusting. This is all wrong." I scratched at my arms in an attempt to occupy my hands, to break flesh, to feel anything other than that twisted knot of anger. It didn't work.

The old homeless woman was worse than my parents. She ignited that knot worse than they ever could.

I remembered how hard I willed it to disappear as I plunged that knife deep into my mother's chest. How badly I hoped that it would end it, stop that festering knot from ever returning.

The woman looked me in the eyes and smiled. The smile made my skin crawl, I hated her, but I forced myself to look back. I looked at her. *Really looked at her.* It took me a moment to notice, but eventually I recognised my own eyes staring back at me. Even shrouded in all those wrinkles, they were mine.

I thought of the dead bodies of my parents and the fate that awaited me for my actions. I realised that the woman lied, she wasn't free. She never had been. She was me, and she scared me more than anything else could.

That same festering pit existed in her, too. She'd run from it for years, hiding from the consequences of her actions, and she had the audacity to taunt me? She didn't say another word. She didn't have to.

I only had one more question for her. *For me.*

"It's been nice to meet you, Sophie. What are you avoiding going home to?"

MY BOY TEDDY

I had a family. A wife and a little boy. Rebecca and Teddy. Before it happened, I often wondered how anyone got over the loss of a child; but losing a child followed by the suicide of a soul mate wasn't a pain that I'd ever considered.

My son always smiled. He had curly, wild blonde hair and bright blue eyes that looked straight out of a Disney cartoon. He loved playing with trucks and he told us he loved us every day. That's the boy I want to remember.

Teddy was murdered.

He didn't die in a car accident or fall off the top of a piece of playground equipment. I sometimes wish it had been that senseless. Would it have made it less painful to know it was a random, tragic accident and not a real person squeezing the last breath from my 5-year-old son's throat?

Maybe. Probably not.

I think Rebecca would've found it less painful if she hadn't hired the babysitter who snuck her murderous boyfriend in. If she'd been a little more thorough in the vetting process and not so desperate for date night, maybe Teddy would be alive. Maybe *she* would be alive, too. I wish I could've taken some of that pain from her before it was too late, but if I'm honest, I blamed her too.

You can't comfort a person you can't bear to look at.

It's miserable. Tiny coffins are the kind of thing that haunt your dreams. They haunted Rebecca. That star covered miniature box was probably the last thing she thought of before she did it.

She didn't leave a note. What was the point? She'd apologised a thousand times, and I'd pretended to forgive her even more. She didn't leave a note because there was nothing more to say.

I mourned her... I still do. But as they lowered her coffin, all I could think of was the one my son laid in, a fraction of the fucking size. I loved her and I hated her but most of all I resented her. She got to run away from that tiny, star spattered box.

It's tragic, but it isn't why I'm here. My intention isn't to make any of you pity me. Grief took me to some dark places, and I thought I'd come through the other side. It never gets better, but you learn to bear it. Or in my case drink until it's quiet.

Before I lost my family, I had a successful career in I.T. Boring as it sounds, I loved the job. To try to distract myself through the months that followed Rebecca's passing, I spent a lot of time holed up in my room with the curtains closed, on websites, reading technology journals, forums and eventually conspiracy theories. A fucked-up mind and litres of alcohol really fuels that kind of thing.

That's how I came across the concept of a *deep fake*.

For those who don't know, a deep fake is an artificial image or video of a real person, created by an AI that uses existing images to learn every angle of the face, perfectly replicating the real thing. It's a technology that's been used to bring dead actors back to life in film and in stark contrast, to create revenge porn and blackmail people.

I don't know if it were the half litre of whiskey attacking my liver or the grief, but while staring at the pages and pages of discussion on the topic of deep fakes, I started to wonder if I could bring my son back. Digitally.

It sounds crazy, I know. But unless you've lost a child, you wouldn't understand the pain. The longing for just one more second with them. I thought I could use my aptitude for technology to give myself just a few more minutes of his beautiful face. Was it selfish? Yes.

Show me a parent in my position who wouldn't do the same.

I had hundreds of photos and videos, but the idea of a totally new one was special. My son moving in front of me, even if it was just through a screen, even if it wasn't entirely real, it didn't matter. A whole new memory to cherish. A stolen moment clawed back.

Fascination became obsession. I spent days researching, hacking and downloading all the correct programs. I meticulously selected my best photographs and videos of Teddy; ones with the sharpest images to give the technology the best shot at working. I cried over them. Every single one.

I thought about Rebecca too. I wondered how it would feel to face her again, to feel all the emotions I'd buried. I thought about it, but I didn't do it. I wasn't prepared for those kinds of complex emotions. I just wanted my son back.

And it worked.

After days of agonising there he was. In my computer screen. Those cute little blonde ringlets against a stark, artificial, white background were unmistakable. The setting didn't matter, it was Teddy. I sobbed for hours as he blinked and smiled back at me.

It didn't feel how I'd expected to. It wasn't like watching a video of my poor, dead son. It was more like he was stood in front of me. As absurd as it is, I was certain he was reacting to me, smiling to comfort at intervals, giggling to cheer me up.

I'd only intended to create a few minutes of footage, but the longer I looked the more alive he became. I couldn't bear to let him go. Not again. I kept going until my eyes just refused to stay open.

I woke up in the early hours, cheek pressed against the beeping keyboard. There was an instant panic, like all the air had been sucked out of my lungs. Like I'd lost him all over again. But when I raised my head, those blue eyes were still staring back at me.

Except this time they were filled with tears.

I hadn't used unhappy footage. I hadn't programmed him to cry. It shouldn't have been happening, but it was.

"Teddy." I sighed as the tears rolled down his plump little cheeks. He shook his head in distress, just like the real thing had always done when he was alive. I wanted so badly to scoop him up and hold him. My heart felt too full, I realised the whole exercise had probably been a mistake, all I'd done was ripped open a fresh wound.

Daddy.

His voice. It wasn't like a computer-generated falsification. It was him. I tried to write it off, he probably said Daddy in a lot of the videos. The programme must have ripped it from those... but he sounded so upset. The wobble in his tone was so distinctive. I'd never made a habit of filming my boy in tears, I would comfort him instead.

"What's wrong, buddy." I asked, struggling to get my words out, feeling ashamed for talking to a screen.

Daddy, I'm stuck!

Teddy sobbed and raised his little fists before hitting out at the screen from inside it. What was left of my swollen heart sunk into my stomach. This was sick. Some sort of deep fake programming trick that I was too inexperienced to explain. It was a hard decision, but the experience was no longer cathartic. I had to nuke the programme for my own sanity.

I raised a hand to the screen and artificial Teddy opened one of his fists to match it. I could barely see, as overwhelming tears cascaded from my eyes and I tried to imagine the feel of my son's fingers against my own instead of the cold glass. One deep breath.

Then I did it; I killed the programme and watched in anticipation.

Nothing happened. Teddy was still there. No matter what pattern of keys I pressed or where I clicked the mouse he remained. Crying. Only, after my attempts to stop, he looked even more distressed. Like he was in pain.

Daddy, please help me I'm stuck and it hurts! Please help me!

The heart sitting in my stomach ripped into pieces inside me. I screamed. I tried to hold it in, but I couldn't. I'd spent so long holding it in. I had to be there for Rebecca, had to hold it together while that tiny coffin lowered. Had to hold it together when I found *her* and then when I buried her too.

No more. The floodgates were open.

My skin crawled and my son sobbed as I pulled the plug on the computer. I saw no other option. I couldn't take his pain. Was that how he cried before that man… it doesn't even bare thinking about. Finally, after what felt like forever, the screen went black and Teddy was gone. I was left with an empty, silent life once again, this time with an extra, exceptional pain.

I hid under my duvet, scrunching my eyes hoping things would go black, but behind them was him. Against that stark, white background. In tears. Was this the last memory I would have of my son? Did my selfishness taint what little happy memories I had? It was impossible to sleep.

I almost missed the sounds of my phone over my loud and invasive thoughts. But a parent knows their kid's voice and even after they die, the instinct never goes away.

Daddy, please help me!

I lifted the phone in horror. My usual lock screen photograph of him was gone. Replaced by a moving image against white. The same moving image I'd just desperately destroyed on my computer. The same image that was back on the unplugged computer screen again. His little fists pounding against yet another screen, begging me for freedom. What the fuck had I done?

I fled the house with nothing, I tried so hard to run away from my son. *My son.* Who was begging for my help. It's cowardly, running away. But I was out of my depth and I didn't have a clue what to do. So I just ran.

Whatever I've created isn't going away. What I did worked all too beautifully. I did manage to bring my son back, but it came at a huge price. He's in my phone, my computer, my television and he's on every screen I pass in the street.

Everywhere I go he follows. Pounding his fists against the glass. He's in the corner of my phone now, while I type this, in a small box that I can minimise but I can't destroy. The longer it goes on, the more distressed he gets. Not long ago he started head butting the screen. I begged him to stop, but he won't. He just keeps repeating the same words.

Daddy. Help. Get me out.

I can't take it. I'm not strong enough to take it. Rebecca got to run away, she got to end it all before it got to this. I've never been religious, but I'm hoping that I was wrong. That somewhere, they're together and no one's crying. It's a beautiful thought.

I don't know what the chances are of that being the case, but anything has to be better than this, right? Anything. Even if it's just black, it's better than watching him suffer.

What happened to Teddy has made me wonder. What about all those actors they bought back? The other deep fakes that have been created over the years. Are they all trapped? All in the type of pain that my son is?

I wish I had the strength to find out. But I can't do it anymore. I'm going home to my family.

A LATE-NIGHT DOG WALK

Charles slept. Just like he always did. Snoring away, his sounds kept me awake like a taunt. Mocking me with how wonderful it must have felt to sleep that deeply. It had been a long time since I'd slept like that.

Robert scratched at the door. I know. Who the fuck calls their dog Robert? Charles did. Even though I looked after that dog better than he ever could he was always going to be Charles' baby.

We lived in a flat, no garden. I rolled my eyes in the dark room, knowing I would have to get dressed and take Robert through the park opposite. I'm not ashamed to admit that I cursed that dog. It was so late, and I was so pregnant.

My jacket wouldn't do up over my belly. It amazed me that Charles slept soundly through all the kerfuffle. Me rustling for poop bags and Robert excitedly tippy tapping around the flat. I did consider that he might feign unconsciousness to avoid the walk, but his low, rumbling snores said otherwise.

I wouldn't have even chanced it this late in this neighbourhood if it weren't for Robert. I was a five foot nothing, eight-month pregnant lady and the ideal prey for some degenerates that found their entertainment on the streets. But even those types don't tend to bother someone walking a hundred kilo mastiff.

Robert was a soppy fucker. Wouldn't hurt a fly. Mostly because he lacked the coordination to catch them. Others didn't need to know that though, which is why I opted for the thick chain leash for my late-night walk. It looked more intimidating.

The park was small but surrounded by thick borders of trees that created enough of a canopy to eclipse any light pollution from the lampposts outside it. I readied the torch on my phone as I felt that strange illusion you feel in darkness.

You know the one, right? When even open eyes feel closed.

The torch only illuminated a small patch, but it was enough for me to follow Robert on the path through the trees. I'll be the first to admit that the situation made me uneasy, but it was better than how uneasy my stomach would've been had Robert pissed on the floor at home.

Every breeze felt like a monster weaving through the trees to touch me. I clutched the lead so tight I'm sure my knuckles would've been white if I could see them. Something about being alone in the dark had sparked that strange primal fear that we all understand. Fear of the unknown. The abyss.

Once that fear had set in, I couldn't shake it. I silently willed Robert to find a place he wanted to do his business so we could get the fuck home. My heart rate increased. I experienced the irrational feeling that I was being watched. Followed even.

Ridiculous.

I lifted my torch to light the area in front of me and did an entire 360 turn to ensure that I was alone. I was. I knew I was. No one likes the dark, do they? It's human nature. We aren't designed to be outside in the dark, no adapted night vision or echo location like the species that thrive in it.

I think that's where the fear originates.

Finally, the lead pulled tight. Prince Robert had finally found a patch that he deemed worthy of a toilet. The trickling sound was like music to my hyper vigilant ears.

I stood and looked up to the stars for a few moments while I waited for the dog to finish. The sky was totally clear, stars littering every inch. It was a far less disconcerting sight than the thick black tree outlines that danced and had littered my peripherals throughout the walk.

I rustled in my pocket for a poop bag. Making even the faintest of sounds sent my anxiety sky high again. I kept a protective hand on my belly. As if the non-existent being who had followed me earlier was going to jump at me now that I'd drawn attention.

Ridiculous. That's what I kept telling myself. I told myself that right up until I lifted my torch to face the area that Robert had stopped.

Until I saw *her*.

The girl sat there. Crossed legged in the pitch black, unfazed by the blinding light, I was now shining directly in her pale brown eyes. Her face was etched with fear, worry lines cutting deeply through her forehead, framed perfectly by her long, centre parted dark hair.

I gasped, swallowing a scream. Her body language didn't match the fear on her face, her posture was like that of a ballerina, stoic and proud despite her childlike crossed legs. One arm was outstretched almost poker straight, gently stroking Robert behind the ears with her long, pale fingers.

I tried to fathom why a girl would sit alone in a dark wooded area like this. Did she feel safe amongst nature? Or was she lost? She made me so uncomfortable I wanted to run.

"Are you ok?" I called out, tugging on the lead to usher Robert away from her without taking a single step closer. Not a word. Nothing.

"Excuse me? Miss… are you ok?" I tried again.

She didn't respond, but the worry lines on her face started to twist and contort along with her lower jaw into a falsified, forced looking smile. I felt my heart drop. Robert edged backwards, tail between his legs, but she kept her arm outstretched straighter than should've been possible.

As he finally backed away enough that she couldn't reach his fur any longer, she got up. The speed that she moved shouldn't have been possible… it certainly wasn't typical human movement.

I'm not sure I even caught her uncrossing her legs before she was stood, malnourished frame looming, and eyes fixed on my own; regardless of the fact she shouldn't have been able to see them in the darkness. Her hair draped all the way to her thin waist, dirty and unwashed.

She turned and sprinted into the trees with enough velocity that branches were propelled in all directions. With her stature, I was amazed she could move at all. I could've sworn she went upwards, into the canopy, but my torch didn't cover that much distance.

Soon she was out of sight completely.

I could feel my heart in my throat pounding, and my hands were clammed up into fists. My baby kicked hard, reminding me I had an entire life to consider. I needed to get the fuck out of there quickly.

My mind raced with all explanations for what I'd just seen. Each one wilder than the next as I power walked Robert back through the park home. I struggled to think of anything benign. At best the girl was a victim of human trafficking set out to lure others, at worst a demon out to hunt me.

It sounds extreme. But I was so overcome with that primal, irrational fear that my head wouldn't go anywhere else. I inhaled deeply as I reached the exit, and the beautiful glow of the streetlamps drew my focus. I realised I must have been holding my breath for quite some time as I panted on the quiet street.

I'd never quite felt a panic like it. A stationary girl that stroked my dog and ran away. I could already hear Charles making fun of me for being so scared, but damn, I was fucking scared. And standing under that light, opposite the apartment building I called home, bought with it a genuine relief.

I crouched a little and cuddled Robert. I never wanted a dog, but he was special. I was glad Charles had bought him into my life and even more relieved that he was by my side through my ordeal.

As I prepared to cross the road, there was an ear-piercing whistle. I instinctively clutched both ears with my hands, letting go of Robert's leash. He wasn't usually one to run off. He'd have walked by my side no matter what, the lead was more for other's peace of mind than ours.

He wasn't usually one to run off. I swear it. But he ran.

Robert bolted straight back into the park, towards the whistle. I tried to follow, but it was no use. My swollen ankles were no match for the beastly dog. I felt the heart rate rise again. The awful, sinking feeling in the pit of my stomach returned as the light behind me faded again.

I couldn't go any further. I loved that dog. I'd have followed him anywhere, but instead I was hit by a reluctance in my entire body to take even a single step further into the park.

I backed away, the pounding of my heart intensified until I reached the exit once more and I could feel a thumping pain in my entire body. Then I heard it. That trickle.

Had Robert come back?

I fumbled my phone in my hands, missing the torch button multiple times before it finally switched on. The trickle hadn't come from Robert. He wasn't anywhere to be seen. It had come from the liquid that was leaking out of me and now drenching my jeans.

Not now. It was too early. Just not now. Fuck.

They were the last thoughts that ran through my mind as I stumbled out onto the street. The pain was unbearable, so intense. The light that starkly contrasted the park dimmed. I called out for Charles.

Everything went black.

***

I woke in the hospital. Machines beeping, Charles smiling at my bedside with tears in his eyes and blinding artificial lighting from above.

The panic started all over.

"Is the baby ok!?" I blurted, desperate.

"She's perfect." He answered, gushing as he moved to the side to show me the tiny cot behind him, with my perfect newborn daughter inside. "A little early, but she's strong. Didn't need any help breathing or anything. It was you we've all been worried about."

I couldn't organise my thoughts properly. I wanted desperately to hold my baby, to start bonding with her and to choose a name that suited her little face… I could see that she looked like me… But I had to ask.

"Did you find Robert?"

Charles' face dropped, and I knew the answer before he spoke.

"James is out looking. He's searched the whole park, but he can't find him so he's gonna get some posters made up. I'm surprised, I thought he'd have stood and guarded you in distress like that." Charles looked truly upset at the idea that Robert had left me, but I knew better. He didn't leave me; he ran towards something.

"What happened?" I asked. Realising I couldn't recall a single detail of my own child's birth.

"Mrs. Mosely on the ground floor heard a commotion outside, she went out to see what was happening… What were you doing out there so late, Kay?"

"Robert had to pee. You were asleep."

"I'm so sorry." He sighed with guilt. I could see that he felt responsible for the whole situation, but images of the stoic girl plagued my thoughts. "Mosely said that there was a girl with you, just standing over you stroking your hair. She said that the girl ran as soon as she spotted her, so Mosely called the ambulance in case she hadn't to be sure."

I felt my hands clench into fists. I couldn't enjoy the first moments I spent with my beautiful daughter. Instead, they were filled with that unshakeable primal fear that was starting to feel like a permanent state.

"I have to pee. Please Charles." I didn't. I just wanted a moment to myself.

He helped me steady myself to stand and make my way to the corner of the room and into my hospital bathroom. I shut the door behind me and wept, both for Robert and for how tarnished this milestone had been.

I didn't want Charles to see me cry, I rubbed my eyes and approached the mirror. What I saw in my reflection sparked something much stronger than the primal fear of the dark. It was genuine terror, and it smacked me in the face.

Written in the condensation was a message. Just for me.

I took your dog. I'll be back for the baby.

LETTERS TO ANNABELLE

Dear Annabelle,

I wanted to take a moment to apologise for the last time we spoke. I've not been in a very good place lately and when I hung up, it wasn't because of you. That's why I thought I'd try writing instead. I miss you and maybe this way we can talk without me frightening you. I never meant to do that.
    I hope you don't mind.
    Things have been bad. I guess you already knew that, but they've gotten worse. Larry left after the incident, so I had to find a new roommate. His name is Artis, he's a student and he loves to party. He and his friends do a lot of drugs, so I try to stay out of his way. I don't want to go back down that road. We aren't clicking but I really need his half of the rent, so I have to put up with it.
    Work is bad too. My boss realised that I'd been a little out of sorts and now he's watching me like a hawk. Feels kinda claustrophobic. Sometimes I really want to tell him where to stick it but I'm trying to be calmer these days. I want another chance at life. Maybe another chance to be part of your life. I'd like that, Annabelle, really.
    Anyway, I should stop rambling. How are you? How are the kids? Have they asked about me?
    I'm so sorry.

D.

***

Dear Annabelle,

I know you asked me not to write you again, but I need to talk to you. We're meant to be family, I know what I did was wrong but you can't just ignore me like this, surely?

Don't you remember when mum and dad would argue and we'd build a fortress out of pillows and pretend they weren't there? I thought we'd be that close forever.

Artis got arrested this weekend. Police searched the house and found all his drugs. They're not charging me with anything because I was so pathetic when they found me cowering in my room, I was so relieved they didn't call me in.

I'd built a pillow fortress to hide in just like we used to.

They didn't find the box. That's what I needed to tell you. That no matter how bad things are for me or between us I won't let anyone find that box. I'm a good brother.

You don't need to answer this. You can tear it up if you want.

Just know that I love you.

D.

***

Annabelle,

I think it's pretty heartless that you're still ignoring me. Just putting that out there. When I said that I wished John would get hit by a truck it was just a throwaway comment. Coincidences happen. I don't want you telling the kids I'm some kind of monster. You know that's not the case.

When you read this, remember all the times we sat and read stories together. I wish you'd let me read stories to Mina and Joey. I'm their uncle... your little brother. You're meant to love me no matter what.

Artis made bail. He was back home within a few days and we had a big argument. I asked him to leave and he didn't want to. Eventually we compromised. He's staying, but only on my terms. He's been much quieter. No drugged-up visitors. It's nice. For a few days it's been like things are looking up.

I spend a lot of time in my pillow fortress.

I've been thinking about that box a lot since my last letter. Even if you didn't answer me, I know you're thinking about it too. What's inside it isn't just my fault, you know. It's yours too.

You can't pretend I don't exist forever.

D.

***

Annabelle,

FUCK YOU. *That's* all you had to say? That everything is my fault?! One sentence. One fucking sentence is all you could spare for your brother? You called me a freak. Just like John. You know how much I hate that.

Well, I know where I stand now. I know I'm alone. I know that the girl that helped me hide the pieces of OUR childhood mistake is as good as dead. And I'm going to expose it all.

You knew how my mind worked. You knew what I could do, and you manipulated me. I didn't want to hurt anyone. You were older. Mum and dad were barely home and when they were they were drinking and screaming. YOU were my mother. And you've abandoned me.

This is all YOUR fault. My life's fucked. I don't care what happens to me. I'm posting the box to the police with your return address attached.

John paid for calling me a freak and taking you all away from me and now you'll pay, too.

D.

***

Dear Annabelle,

I didn't mean what I said.

I never do. You know that. I'm not going to say I'm sorry anymore because it won't make any difference. It didn't make any difference when Kayla was on the floor bleeding, and it won't make any difference now.

You told me that you hated her, that you didn't want her around. I was a kid and I got confused. I never wanted her to die. She was our sister too you know, even if she thought our pillow forts were lame.

You saw what happened to that kid that picked on you at school... all the blood. I know you don't believe me, but I never touched them. I didn't touch that kid, and I didn't touch Kayla. I hurt them... with my mind.

It was all for you, Annabelle. All of it.

I know John meant a lot to you, but he didn't know you like I do. You need me to get through this. Please. Please let me come home. Artis hasn't been paying his rent, and I'm going to lose my place real soon.

I'm begging.

D.

***

Dear Annabelle,

I got the message. Well... the lack of message. Don't say I didn't give you a chance to fix this.

I'm not sorry.

D.

***

The preceding letters were found neatly stacked in date order, next to the body of Annabelle Laker. The widowed mother of two was found by the police having hung herself in her locked bathroom. Her children were hungry and distressed in the living room and had been alone for a number of hours.

Police entered after receiving a box with a severed finger bone matching the DNA profile of a missing girl whose case had long gone cold, the deceased's sister, Kayla Carlson. When officers arrived at the property, there was no answer at the door and the sound of crying children. Forced entry was made. The box came from an anonymous source that we strongly suspect is the writer of the letters.

Attempts have been made to contact "D", but no forwarding address was available and there was no record or evidence of Mrs. Laker ever having a brother.

We searched the registered property of the missing person, Artis Thackery, but found no evidence of another person living there. Police spoke to a roommate of Mr. Thackery's when he was arrested prior to his disappearance, but the roommate gave the name Abel, and was not deemed a person of interest in that particular case. As a result, officers did not take a last name and we have not been able to locate him.

One final letter was found; pinned to Mrs. Laker's body with a thumbtack. We have decided to make it public in the hope it will appeal to the intended recipient, and that he will come forward with whatever information he has in this highly unusual case.

Daniel/Abel/D, if you are reading this, we want to speak to you as a matter of urgency. Please present yourself at the nearest police station.

***

Dear Daniel,

I'm sorry. I am. Even if you aren't anymore. I know I've never acknowledged this before, but I knew exactly what you were capable of when I goaded you into hurting Kayla. That's why I always protected you. I knew that I ruined two lives that day.

This is my confession. Her blood is on both our hands.

I'm sorry I abandoned you. You have to understand how badly I wanted a family? Surely? If anyone was going to understand that it, was you. I wanted you to be a part of it more than anything, but John couldn't get past his reservations. I had to put the kids first. After what happened to Larry's girlfriend, I knew things would never change. John insisted I cut you off.

I didn't expect you to get so volatile.

I know you won't understand. No one will. No one knows you like I do. No one knows what you can do like I do. I don't want the kids to grow up in a world where I've abandoned my blood and I don't want them to grow up knowing how much blood has been spilled because of me.

I know you've sent the box. I know it's only a matter of time before the police are at my door.

I never knew why you kept that thing. I just knew it gave me the creeps. What kind of person keeps a part of a person like that? I don't know what you gained from that. I'm meant to be honest here, right? You are creepy Daniel... you know that don't you.

I saw the article about Artis. Do you think I don't read the news? He didn't quieten down after his arrest did he? He argued with you and he died. Just like they all do. That's why he's missing. That's why his family have been crying on the television. Just like our parents did. I wonder what part of him you kept.

Even when you write me, you continue to bullshit your way into victimhood. But how many boxes are there?

Kayla may be partly my fault, but what about all the others? The kid who taunted me, Larry's girlfriend, Artis.... John. They all died because of you. You aren't a kid anymore, Daniel, and you can't hide in a pillow fortress forever.

You called me your mother and you were right. I should be spending my last moments talking to my children, but instead here I am, spilling my guts to you.

You're like a parasite I just can't get rid of.

And that's why I'm going to die. If I can't get rid of you, then no one around me is safe... so I have to get rid of me.

Despite everything, I'll always love you.

A.

DON'T FORGET TO FEED THE FISH

When I was eight years old, I forgot to feed my pet fish and it died. I cried. It was the worst thing I'd ever done in my short life. The guilt was immeasurable.

It's a moment I've come back to every time I've got it right or wrong in my life. A defining moment. I can't help but wonder who I might've been if I'd remembered to feed that fish.

When I was twelve years old, I hit a girl. I liked her and asked her on a date. She was my first crush and she turned me down. I was humiliated on the playground in front of all my peers. So I hit her.

It was terrible, but it's the truth. Maybe if I'd remembered to feed that fish, I could've showed her my cool pet and she would've liked me.

When I was sixteen years old, I cheated on my girlfriend. I think the girl that turned me down had ruined my perspective of women because I didn't treat them well. I wasn't very good with people in general. I cheated on her, but worst of all I cheated with her mother.

I'd never seen someone quite as broken as she was when she found us. Maybe if I'd remembered to feed that fish then I would've learned how to take care of other living things better. Maybe I wouldn't have hurt her.

When I was eighteen years old, I stole from my grandparents. I had developed a nasty drug habit and I found money wherever I could. I did arguably worse things to feed the habit, but the theft from them was the most morally bankrupt.

I felt guilt, but in the throes of my addiction I had no restraint. Maybe if I'd remembered to feed that fish, I would've had a different hobby. Maybe I would've occupied my time with home aquariums instead of drugs.

When I was twenty-five years old, I met my wife. Her name was Rosa and we met in recovery. She pulled all the darkness out of my life. Even though we had both been to the most hopeless places, finding each other was a beacon of light. She was the first woman that I truly cared for.

I'd never quite felt anything like it. Maybe if I'd remembered to feed that fish, I wouldn't have ever met Rosa. Maybe keeping it alive would've been the real tragedy.

When I was twenty-seven, I got married and we had our first child. A boy named Freddie. I had always imagined my life going to shit, instead I was living a beautifully mundane existence.

When we bought Freddie home from the hospital he cried and cried. He kept us up for days. I fed him, held him, rocked him, and barely let him out of my sight for even a second.

My son became my world, and I didn't want him to go without anything he needed. Maybe if I remembered to feed that fish, I would never have learned the consequences of neglect. Maybe I would've been a terrible dad.

When I was twenty-eight years old, Rosa bore our second child. A girl we named Emilia. She was beautiful, just like my wife. I felt like Emilia sucked all the life out of Rosa because soon my soulmate was a shell of herself.

Wiped out, empty, all the vitality gone. She wasn't a person that I recognised, and my daughter became a source of resentment. I could swear on my whole family that Emilia was amused by her mother's despair. Even as a newborn she was only calm when her mother wept.

I tried to love Emilia like I did Freddie. It just wasn't possible. Maybe if I remembered to feed that fish, I would've known how to help Rosa, I would've learned how to perk up someone who's struggling. Maybe I wouldn't have learned to just ignore the issue.

When I was thirty years old, I became a single father and a widow. Rosa couldn't bear the pain anymore and took her own life. I hate to admit it, but I found it selfish. She left me alone with my perfect son and the spawn of Satan, knowing that I wasn't emotionally equipped to cope.

Emilia terrified me. It sounds ridiculous to say that about a two-year-old, but it's true. There was something sinister about that girl. She didn't mourn her mother in any capacity. She never asked for her or cried for her like her brother did. In fact, she never really cried at all after Rosa's death.

I started drinking again. I didn't do drugs, but the drink was a big enough threat to my sobriety. I became a useless father. Maybe if I remembered to feed that fish, I would've learned a lesson about commitment. About not giving up on those who depend on you.

When I was thirty-two years old, my four-year-old daughter attacked her brother with a kitchen knife. I was drunk and hadn't been watching them. It was my fault... Or was it hers? She giggled with such glee as the blood poured from his screaming face.

Freddie was ok, but he was scarred for life. They were taken off me not long after. When social services got involved, I told them all about Emilia, about how I didn't trust her and how much she frightened me... how I blamed Rosa's death on her. They looked at me as if I were positively insane.

Seeing Freddie maimed and taken from me tore my heart to pieces, but I'll be the first to admit that I was relieved not to have *that other child* in my house. It's an awful thing to say about your own daughter, but I just knew that she was pure evil.

Maybe if I'd remembered to feed that fish, I could've taught my kids about caring for others. Maybe I should've gotten them a fish.

When I was thirty-six years old, I got a call to say that my daughter had been involved in a serious incident in foster care. I'd cleaned up my act, fought the courts and won back my son. I kept in touch with the nice lady that ran the home Emilia lived in, but we mutually agreed it was best for her and Freddie that she didn't come home.

Emilia had drowned the hamster that the kids at the home shared. My eight-year-old daughter had killed an animal. I felt a deep disdain for her, but I couldn't vilify her for the act. She was just like me. That damn fish.

She had told her carers that she was just trying to bathe it. The nice lady was naïve, but I could hear in her voice that she wasn't convinced by Emilia's story. She was as scared as I had been, but neither of us wanted to acknowledge it. So we never did.

I left that woman to live with my problem without warning. Maybe if I remembered to feed that fish, then that hamster wouldn't have drowned. Maybe my whole family would be stood round a beautiful aquarium, pointing out their favourites. Maybe Rosa would still be alive.

When I was thirty-nine years old, I got a call to say that Emilia had run away from the foster home after attacking another child. The attack was serious enough that the police were searching for her.

I had been less involved in her life as the years went by. To be honest, I'm surprised they even called me at all, but they wanted to know if a message she left had any significance. It did, but I wasn't sure where to even begin, so I kept quiet.

Emilia had pinned down a younger child and carved a drawing into their back before jumping from a second-floor window to escape. Maybe if I remembered to feed that fish then that poor child wouldn't have to live with a crudely drawn fish on their back.

When I was forty years old, I accepted that my life was over. Emilia was coming for me, and it was only a matter of time. I sent my previous son to live with his grandmother, Rosa's mother. All that time spent fighting for him and I was sending him away.

It was for the best. I could see the resentment in his eyes. A paranoid, recovering addict dad who couldn't handle his baby sister. A dad who had allowed him to be disfigured. I understood why he was so willing to go.

Waiting for her to show up had been all consuming. I'd pulled him out of school. Installed more deadlocks than I could count. Quizzed him every day on strangers he'd seen or noises he'd heard. When he left with his suitcase, I could breathe. He would be safe.

Maybe if I remembered to feed that fish, then it wouldn't be coming back to haunt me. It wouldn't have ruined my entire life. But it was just a fish... and I was just a kid. I didn't understand the impact of my actions. It wasn't fucking fair.

I'm forty-two years old now. The police have stopped looking for my daughter. They say that they haven't, but they have. An eleven-year-old girl exposed to the elements wasn't expected to last long. I might have been forgetful, I might have forgotten about the fish, but I wasn't stupid. She would be fourteen now. They all presume her dead.

Common sense would implore anyone to feel the same. What a tragedy; a young life plagued with mental disturbance and misery, a dead mother, violent outbursts and a useless dad, ending in a cold death in nature. Or worse, picked up by someone utterly reprehensible.

I know differently. My daughter isn't mentally disturbed at all. She was born evil. I'd often wondered if it was because of that damn fish. Was a higher power punishing me for my cruelty? Was there something bigger than all of us at play? Or was she just a senseless horror that I was unlucky enough to unleash on the world?

Either way, I know she isn't dead. I can feel *her* and she's getting closer. It's been years now and she's bided her time. I can only assume it was to inflict maximum suffering on me, but I think that's finally coming to an end.

Yesterday I got a folded-up piece of paper through the letterbox. It was a child's drawing. It wasn't as sophisticated as you'd expect a fourteen-year-old to produce, but she had been living in the elements for quite some time without further education, so it was hardly surprising.

I wish the subject matter had been surprising. I wish it had shocked me and been something different. But it wasn't. That damn fish has been haunting me my entire life and there I was in blue crayon in a bowl just like the one I'd kept the real one in.

It summed up everything that had ever gone wrong in my life. Every single pain filled moment came down to that fucking fish. I've tried to come up with other reasons, tried desperately to make sense of all the fuck-ups but I can't. Rosa, Freddie, the foster kid… fuck knows how many more lives destroyed over an eight-year-old's poor attention span.

So, while I wait for my daughter to come and slaughter me, I spend my time downing vodka on my kitchen floor; reading her poorly scrawled words over and over.

To Daddy

Don't forget to feed the fish.

From Emilia.

THE HOTEL NEIGHBOUR

Me and my husband are having a rough time at the moment. Our relationship is not the secure place that it usually is. It's a boat swaying side to side just waiting to capsize. I'd rather not talk about why right now, it's still quite raw and painful.

It may feel hopeless, but I really do love him. That's why I'm here, in this beautiful luxury spa hotel in the British countryside. To give us both some space and some time to miss each other.

I arrived 5 days ago, I got my hair done the day before, freshly dyed a shade of auburn—this was different from my usual blonde locks and it made me feel like a whole new person. I needed that, after all the trouble with my husband. Sometimes it's important to be somebody else. Maybe that's why as I checked in I signed a name that was not my own.

Laura Keller. I don't know why I chose that, but I did. My real name was Rose Borne, and everyone knew me for my long blonde hair and devoted husband, John. But for this week, in this hotel, I was solo travelling, flame haired Laura Keller and it felt wonderful.

The man on the desk was incredibly polite as I checked in. I had been used to low-rate hotels and cheap getaways with John. But I used savings to treat myself to this week, I figured I deserved to experience it at least once in my life. I could feel eyes watching me as I paid for my stay and deliberated over how many extra spa treatments I would add on to my package.

As I received my room key and turned around, I was faced with the owner of the eyes that had been burning the back of my head. An incredibly handsome man, quite a bit older than me, but that was familiar to me, John was much older too. I had been only 18 when we wed, 7 years ago. The distinguished gaze and silver but full head of hair of this handsome guest made him so attractive to me. His piercing blue eyes lighting up as he smiled and nodded at me.

I blushed as I smiled back and continued down the corridor to my room. I could still feel my flushed cheeks as I entered my suite, but was soon distracted by the gorgeous accommodation. There were opulent maroon full drop curtains that matched the soft furnishings and sheets on the four-poster bed that was complete with gold details. A huge flat screen television fixed to the wall.

The suite had a balcony and a bathroom complete with hot tub bath and waterfall style shower. The view from the balcony overlooked acres of countryside, bordered by woods in the horizon.

It was bliss. Just what I needed to forget about all the drama at home, the reason I'd left John. The amount of attention he way paying to that stupid girl... no. I'm still not ready to talk about that.

As I laid on the bed with the balcony door open enjoying the breeze there was a knock at my door. I got up slowly, hoping John hadn't found me. I didn't tell him I was coming; I used an email address he didn't know about to book it and everything. I know it sounds paranoid, but I haven't been apart from him in so long I just needed some space. I had no worries about him reporting me missing, we were in such a bad place when I left, he's probably busy courting the next one now.

It wasn't John. It was the handsome stranger from the hotel lobby, his smile was still in place as he looked at me with those blue eyes and asked if I would like to go to dinner with him. My thoughts of John retreated to the smallest crevice of my mind as I accepted his invitation.

His name was Gilbert Thomson. It was an old man's name, but he was only 50, a whole four years younger than John. We talked and we flirted over a three-course gourmet meal in the hotel restaurant and an expensive bottle of wine back in his room.

It turned out that Gil, as he preferred to be called, was my next door neighbour. We made love that night. I know I shouldn't have. I have always been faithful to John and in all honestly have never been intimate with anyone else. John has been everything to me for such a long time now.

Gil was gentle and loving, and seemed to really be interested in what I had to say. John never did, sometimes I think he only married me to keep me. We were physical for a while before we married, and I don't think he wanted to see me move on or be free. He'd had a lot of girls come and go over the years, but he said I was always the special one. I still believe that despite our current position.

After our intimate moment together, Gil left and made the journey to the next room to sleep for the night, the gentleman that he was wanted to let me get a comfortable first night in my suite with no interruption.

I, of course, couldn't sleep, I hadn't slept for a whole week before checking in anyway, but what I had just done to my marriage haunted me along with thoughts of the troubles of home. No number of velvety blankets or dim relaxed lighting could help me drift off.

The next morning I woke up early, I intended to spend the day in the spa and headed out of my room around 7am. As I opened the door, there was Gil, stood smiling at me and directly facing my door, almost as if he had been waiting there. I felt my heart skip a beat, but not in the good way, his smile was not the same. I don't know how to explain it but when someone smiles, they smile with their eyes too. Girls eyes were vacant and expressionless.

"Hi neighbour, I was just passing by! Do you want to join me for breakfast, my treat?" Gil played it off like he hadn't been waiting, but his stance and position gave him away. He had been watching my door.

Despite feeling unsettled by the whole exchange, I agreed to go. After all, I didn't want the only man I had ever slept with besides my husband to be just a one-night stand. A follow up date felt almost obligatory.

At breakfast we talked, we both enjoyed politics and current affairs. Sometimes at home my relationship with John had been so intense that the news was my only connection to the outside world. I didn't work, John provided for us and I rarely left the house. It got lonely, but the news anchors and politicians kept me company.

We were in deep debate about the political climate in the Middle East when Gil let the first strange comment slip out.

"How does your husband feel about that?"

It seems like a simple sentence. But I had committed to my role as Laura Keller at this hotel. I hadn't worn my ring, and I definitely hadn't mentioned my husband. He occupied my every thought, but I was certain that he had not made it into conversation with anyone since I left the house.

Gil had said it with such seriousness. It hadn't been relevant to the conversation, and I was taken aback. He looked at me with the same vacant smile he had at my room door as it left his mouth. When I said I had no husband, he brushed it off, as if he hadn't said that in the first place. It was incredibly strange.

As attractive as I found Gil, he was freaking me out a bit. I had only gotten involved to numb the thoughts of John and it hadn't worked, so there was no point continuing the relationship. I politely thanked him for breakfast and I set about trying to avoid him.

It was an almost impossible task. Everywhere I went, I saw him. My trip to the spa; he was having a treatment as I walked in. My solo reservation in the evening was ruined by him sitting two tables away, smiling at me. He made me feel so uncomfortable and I scorned myself for my actions.

As I sat at the bar after dinner he approached, he asked if he could join me and I politely told him I didn't feel a spark between us and would rather spend some time alone. The next words that came out of his still smiling mouth sent shivers down my spine.

"Well, you are a thorny rose."

It may have been a coincidence. I prayed that it was, but to refer to be by my real name, even if he was talking about the flower, was one hell of a coincidence. Something was wrong with Gil. Twice he had made references to my life that he should be totally unaware of.

He turned and walked away without giving me a chance to respond, and I was left shaken. I waited for half an hour before going back to my room to avoid meeting him outside again. Still, when I reached our corridor, I saw him standing dead still, staring in my direction. As he spotted me, he smiled, nodded, and entered his room. I ran to mine, my hands shaking as I pressed my electronic room key to the pad and shot through the door.

I sat on the floor of my hotel room, back to the door, and cried. This had turned from the escape of a lifetime into feeling trapped by a man. Nothing had changed from being back home. On top of it all I missed John, even after everything he had done to me, everything that happened with that girl, he was my everything. I knew nothing besides him and our life together.

Gil followed me from a distance everywhere. I begged the receptionist to move me to a new room, but they were fully booked. Unsurprising in a hotel of this quality, but disappointing regardless.

All night he bangs on the wall that we share between our neighbouring rooms. I get no more sleep here than I ever did at home with John. I can't go for a swim without him being sat around the pool. I can't eat in the restaurant without his reservation being at the same time as mine and I can't even leave my room without him outside, smiling. He's stopped trying to talk to me.

I'm not sure if it's better now he's silent or worse. It's certainly more unsettling. I can't go home, I'm not ready to see John after what happened despite my concerns about Gil. And now I can't leave my hotel room either.

I've been in here for a day and a half, I put the 24-hour news channel on to soothe myself. It made the whole place feel more like home. And it helps to drown out the banging on the wall that I know is coming from Gil.

This little break has backfired on me badly. I was supposed to relax. Stop thinking about everything that happened. Start again. But Gil has just sent my mind into overdrive, I'm terrified and sleep deprived.

I don't know where to turn anymore. About An hour ago the news flashed up with a new story from my hometown. It was the news that I had been dreading since I left John a week ago. Confirmation that I could never go home again.

Jodie King. The girl that John had been paying all that attention to had been found. Well. Parts of her had been.

Her parents were on the news in tears. I could understand it, their lives had been torn apart, just like their daughter. I felt bad that I was glad she couldn't steal him from me any longer. I felt awful for every limb I removed from her body. I felt bad for still deeply loving John.

I felt bad for running away, but I knew the police would find her. John was at a business conference when I did it and she was in the house. Imagine finding your husband's mistress in your home, the rage. That's what happened, it just bubbled up.

I had suspected John of cheating on me before, but never in our home, and when I saw her, I knew. This wasn't a fling; she was here to stay. She had the same expression on her face that I had when he had first shackled me to the wall and told me I had no parents, no name. The same spark in her eye when she begged me to help her. She was everything he had wanted me to stay forever, and that I couldn't possibly be anymore. He was trying to replace me.

I killed her but the news feature didn't suspect me. The police were called to my husband's house not long after I fled when a human arm was spotted in the rose bushes out front. My rage bred carelessness.

They reported that his wife Rose was missing and presumed to have been killed by him as well.

He was arrested and evidence in the house tied him to 10 other disappearances of young girls ranging from 13 to 17. It was also recently suspected that he was tied to another disappearance of a girl aged 12, 2 years before the others, but no evidence was found. The case just fit his profile perfectly.

The news anchor showed a picture of that little girl before she went missing 13 years ago. Her name was Laura Keller and I fell to the floor and sobbed looking into my own young eyes photographed before I had met John Borne. He had changed my face however he could, but he couldn't change my eyes,

I knew I was looking at a young picture of myself.

It had been such a long time that I had forgotten my life before, but looking at that old picture bought all of my trauma to the forefront in a visceral way. All the things that John had done to me while he was brainwashing me into total devotion, something that had been such a successful venture he was even able to introduce me as his wife in public. I was so dependent that I was given freedoms seldom awarded to anyone considered a hostage.

I wept for my parents, for John, for all the other girls, and most of all for Jodie King. What had I done for such an evil man?

My mind thumped in rhythm with the wall, and I could barely breathe through deep panicked sobs. Everything felt so busy that I barely noticed the thumping stop, and the piece of folded up paper come through the door.

I picked it up and held it at arm's length so that my tears didn't land on it. After not long, the thumping on the wall restarted and it indicated that Gil had been the note leaver and had made it back to his room.

I opened the paper and read the words inside, everyone leaving a bitter lump in my throat that I know will never go away.

*I know what you did. You could have saved her.
I will never let you get a moment's rest.
Gil. T*

THE BLACK CAT

I'd named him Rufus. Cute right? Rufus wasn't mine, but then does a cat really belong to anybody? They're free spirits. I believe they choose their people, and Rufus chose me.

Rufus came at just the right time. Not long after, mine and Tony's arguments got too much. After the trouble happened, the sirens and after he got in the back of that car and left.

Just as I was staring at the bottle of pills on the kitchen side and wondering how much longer I could go on for.

If Tony couldn't live with me, then how could I live with myself?

Meow.

That noise. That single noise saved my life and from that moment on the cat just wouldn't stay away. He visited daily, greeting me at dawn with a loud meow at the kitchen door.

Life was cold and dreary. I lived with a knot in my insides that never went away. The only thing I had to look forward to was Rufus, he brought a light that I'd forgotten even existed. Every morning he trotted across my back garden and waited until I opened the door to give him some attention.

He had no idea how lonely I was. How much I needed that tiny piece of affection.

It was crisp and fresh the morning I received the first note. Rufus was late and I'd started to panic. How sad is that? Standing aimlessly in my kitchen wishing for a cat that wasn't mine just to turn up and say hello.

I sipped that tea so slowly. I wanted to give him as much time as I could, I wanted to believe I hadn't been abandoned. Again.

It came. *Meow.*

I'd never felt relief like it. I opened the door beaming, unable to shake the stupid grin from my face. I looked down at my fluffy friend and crouched to tickle his neck. Tucked between his leather collar and tufty black fur was a folded-up piece of paper.

I can't explain the anxiety I felt. Was it a note from the owner? Did they want me to keep away from their cat? Was someone else feeding him and they were blaming me?

I hated confrontation.

I'd stayed in my own lonely bubble for so long that the thought of communicating with a person gave me palpitations. Shaking, I unfolded the paper.

I know your secret. Are you ready to repent?—a friend.

It was handwritten, not in nice cursive. The handwriting was more of a scrawl than a collection of letters, barely legible. I stood in the garden surveying the rows of houses divided by fences that overlooked my patch of grass.

My stomach churned.

How could they? It had to be a joke. Surely. Some kind of sick prank. They couldn't have known *the secret.*

I thought back to the night of all the trouble, flashes of Tony in the back of my mind, telling me he was sorry, that it would all be ok, him being bundled into the back of the police car. *The guilt.*

I said goodbye to Rufus, placed the note in a drawer, and locked the door behind me.

Someone knew what happened that night. But they couldn't. It was just me and him. He wouldn't tell anyone. Who would listen to a man behind bars anyway?

It was just a prank. It had to be.

The next morning I twirled my spoon in my tea and waited for that familiar *meow*. I'd slept terribly, tossing and turning in a pit of my own inebriated memories of the night it happened. I could feel the bags inflating beneath my eyes.

I felt violated.

My time with Rufus was my personal sanctuary, and now it wasn't the escape it had once been. I should have known that my sins would catch up with me. People like me didn't *deserve* affection.

Meow.

There was Rufus, more paper under his collar. This time that noise wasn't a lifesaver. This time it made me want to pick up that bottle of pills all over again. To end it all.

I scanned the houses, noting a sea of empty windows as I gently pulled the note from beneath the collar and unfolded it, quivering. I ruffled Rufus on the head and tried to swallow the lump in my throat as I backed into my kitchen, bolting the door.

The scrawls were somehow more urgent this time, like the writer had pressed extra hard on the paper, almost tearing it in some places.

There was no more mistaking it for a prank.

Are you really going to let Tony rot for what you did? I told you. I know. Tick tock.

Your friend.

I dropped the note, mouth agape. Was this Tony? Had he gotten sick of the prison food and communal showers and told a buddy or family member what happened? I thought about calling the police, but how could I explain something like that?

I'd have to tell them he took the fall for me that night... I'd be walking myself straight into a cell.

I spent the day in a panic trying to work out what to do. My brain wouldn't function, instead it played a cinematic reel of all the parts of that night I remembered.

The shouting... the drinking... the moment I took my eyes off the road to scream at him a little more.... *the impact.*

I was a sitting duck.

The third morning came, and so did another note. I was a wreck by then, hadn't slept in three days and could barely stay balanced on my feet. I ushered Rufus in, took the note, and shooed him back out.

I wanted to cuddle him, to hold him. Rufus had been such a positive thing in my life. Not anymore, now he just brought fear and pain. Pain that I'd tried so hard to bury.

This time there were jagged tears in the paper, the words extended angrily in places they shouldn't.

You can't hide from me. You and Tony weren't alone that night and you won't silence me any longer. You won't get away with what you did to me...

There was no sign off this time, no mention of being a friend.

I tore it to pieces.

Impossible. It was fucking impossible. The road was empty that night, not a soul for miles. The only other witness... the victim... the girl I didn't see as I turned to scream at Tony... she was dead.

I killed her.

She didn't die on impact, but we knew she was done for, Tony said she couldn't be saved. *That's why we drove away.* Better to preserve two lives than ruin three trying to save one.

That's what he said. I listened. I looked at her, gasping for air on the floor, and I saw my own ruined life. I hate myself for it, I really do. But I didn't *see* her for a second.

That's why we pushed her into the grassy embankment and left her there to die.

The police found the body the next day, already being picked apart by animals at the roadside. I may have killed her, but getting caught was Tony's fault. He was the one that dropped his wallet.

This was his fault!

What a cruel twist of fate that was, to leave your contact details right next to the dead teenage girl. Or was it a valiant act of karma?

I sobbed. I hugged my knees into my chest tightly. Maybe I just needed to come clean? Tell the police that I was the one driving that night, that Tony was just trying to protect me.

Or was it too late? Was it actually *her?* would I even be safe in prison?

I buried my head in the sand. My duvet became my cocoon. I wondered if Tony was eating. Did he regret taking my place?

The next morning I didn't go downstairs. I heard Rufus, mewing beneath my bedroom window, confused as to why he'd been abandoned. It broke me, but I didn't move. I couldn't, I was paralysed. If I never collected the note, then it didn't exist.

I wished that theory had been correct, I really do.

My phone rang, jolting my entire body like an electrocution. I let it ring, determined to wallow in my own guilt. I was doing this to myself, that's what I'd convinced myself. I just needed a day off. The phone reached answerphone and a girl's voice came through the receiver.

"Tick tock... tick tock... tick tock."

I covered my ears with my pillow, but I couldn't sniff it out entirely. She repeated it so many times I started to hum, trying to block it out, but I couldn't.

She was coming for me.

I played that broken memory in my mind again. That argument. I'd been so angry, I was so upset that Tony had been texting someone else, so consumed by it. If I'd never taken my eyes off the road, she would be alive.

That's why he took the fall. The cheating bastard. He was sat in prison for the crime of cheating on his girlfriend. He didn't kill that girl... he didn't veer off that road... he didn't drink six double vodkas before he got behind the wheel.

That was my fault.

"I'm sorry..." I muttered, alone in my room, desperate for whoever it was to hear me. For her to hear me. I had to atone for my sins. I had to confess.

"You're only sorry you got caught." The voice retorted from the answerphone receiver, breaking the incessant repetition of *tick tock*. After that, the line went dead.

I sobbed. I sat in my bed for hours, sobbing and apologising to the air. *I was sorry. I did mean it.*

Hours passed and I waited. There's nothing more frightening in this world than waiting. Waiting for an unknown fate, an unknown vengeance. Unsure if it's the doing of something real or your own guilty mind.

I heard it just after it got dark, the whimpering from outside. I peered out of a small gap in my bedroom curtain, into my back garden.

There she was.

Arms splayed out, bones broken and blood spattered across her clothes. Exactly the same way it was that night, exactly how she looked before we pushed her down the embankment. She wasn't gasping this time though, instead staring right back at me, gently mouthing *tick tock.*

I'm not sure what she's going to do. I know she wants me to suffer, she's biding her time, waiting there with her limbs all mangled; a stark reminder of what I'd done.

Every now and again I peer out that gap in the window, waiting for her next move, but it never comes.

Last time I looked there was Rufus, chewing on her bloodied finger.

NEW YEAR'S EVE, 2020

What a year.

It's not quite the same is it? No photographic round ups of life changing trips away and events. No inspirational messages about what a great year it's been.

No one's had a good 2020. No one. It's been its own global horror that we can all agree on, but that's not what I'm here for.

I'm here because I've had the worst year of my life. I'm here to be selfish. To talk about my fucking self because it might be the last chance I get.

It wasn't just a bad one. And not for the same reasons that yours wasn't so great. I wish the everyday shit show the world has descended into was my main concern, but it just isn't. I've had far stranger things to worry about.

It started in January. Every month it took a little more. Another little piece, chipping away until there's nothing left to take.

January 1st, 2020, I woke up without a left index finger.

It hadn't been cut off, there were no shrewd knife marks and no blood. There was no scar either, it just wasn't there. What do you do when you're missing a digit?

I went to the doctors, pleading with them to work out why I was suddenly missing a finger.

They didn't believe it had ever been there. HA! Right?! Sold me some bullshit line about phantom limbs and a referral to a counsellor.

I begged them to check my records, if I'd been born without it, it would be listed somewhere but my useless mother never took me to the doctors as a kid. The records were barely there. Non-existent, while the doctor was insistent.

I got used to life without a finger. I suppose I had to. Was there really any other choice? It wasn't much of a hindrance, really. It took some adapting but soon I'd learned to write, type and do all kinds of things without the finger.

Maybe the doctor was right? Maybe it was never there to begin with. So I took the counselling referral.

I imagined a finger for 24 years, of course I took it.

6 month waiting list. Wow. I counted every lucky star—and finger—that I wasn't in real psychological distress. What a fucked-up system.

I supposed that I would speak to them when they got to me and kept on going with my life. I didn't know at the time that I was already swimming against an ever increasing current.

February 23rd, 2020, I woke up missing the other index finger. The one on my right hand. It was there the night before, I swear.

I remembered the month I'd spent adjusting, how that finger was dominant as I typed, and how I'd used it for… *pleasurable purposes* just hours earlier. I would not be duped this time.

Terrified, I called the doctor's surgery so many times my phone almost glitched that morning. I managed to get an appointment, a miracle after all the attempts it had taken just to get to reception.

Doc was stumped too. No pun intended. He referred me for blood tests and sent me to a local hospital to be checked over. They didn't find a damn thing.

It was only a few weeks before March 13th came. It was a Friday. You don't forget a Friday 13th, especially not one in 2020, especially not one that rocks your world and changed your life forever.

No. You don't forget the day you wake up without a foot.

A whole foot. My entire left fucking foot was gone. No scar, no cut, no blood, just a clean nub where my ankle should have been. I screamed. I screamed alone in my house and no one came.

I dialled the ambulance, was rushed in for more testing, and they even kept me overnight. I laid in that hospital bed praying for answers. I'm not religious, but if anyone was up there, I was imploring them to help me.

Please. Why couldn't someone just help me.

The staff at the hospital found nothing. They took so much blood I thought I might shrivel and they did everything they could to find the source of the problem. I practically lived at the hospital for weeks.

Weeks that cost me my job. No, you can't fire someone for being sick, or disabled, but you can make them redundant in their first year as the hospitality industry takes a slow dive.

So I was sent home with a prosthetics referral, no job and no foot. Only eight fingers remained.

That's when the depression hit. The sad realisation that I was being affected by some awful disease or condition I never knew about. Disappearing piece by piece.

Then the world collapsed.

By April 20th I was locked down in my apartment, something I considered a tiny miracle if only because my landlord couldn't evict me. Losing my job killed my social life and losing my foot killed my ability to move around a great deal.

It had been so much harder to adapt to than the loss of my fingers.

I took a nap at around 3pm on April 20th, 2020 and woke up an hour later without my right hand.

I sobbed. I panicked. I felt my heart pound and missing fingers twitch. *Maybe this was that phantom limb thing the doctor spoke about.* The nub sat perfectly at the wrist, smooth and purposeful.

I must have wailed in my bed for a week before I called anyone. I was so tired. So disenfranchised. I was falling apart piece by piece and being forgotten at the same rate; I still had no answers.

I called my mum.

I called her. Even after everything she put me through, everything that she ruined for me. We hadn't spoken in five years and I called my mum crying. I barely got my words out, explaining what was wrong and trying to articulate what was happening to me.

You were always rotten. Now you're rotting away.

That was all she said before she hung up. Before the line went dead and I heard the last human voice that I would hear all month.

I was defeated.

I dwelled in bed with her words playing over and over in my mind, like a broken recording of the worst sound you could imagine. I believed her. I gave up.

May 15th, 2020, I woke up missing a breast. Yes. Really. I clutched at my uneven chest, hand sweating as I fumbled with my phone in the other. I still had no job and the little money the government gave me didn't cover it, so I couldn't call my doctor. The only number I could dial was 999.

The ambulance came and they checked me over, they gave me a bed for the night but they couldn't think of anything to do. They took x-rays, more blood tests, and a kindly nurse snuck me £50 to top up my phone so I could call my doctor.

The pandemic had changed everything, I was rushed out of hospital and sent home. Back to my four walls. To the same four walls. To my cell.

June 27th, 2020, I woke up 25 years old. 25 years old and missing the pinkie finger on my remaining hand.

Happy fucking birthday to me.

I shed a tear. Poured a glass of whisky and drank it. Cry. Pour. Repeat. I drank myself into oblivion with all the dregs of alcohol that remained in my cupboard. I sat alone and I toasted every missing piece of me.

The next few months went by and I lost more. I lost my home, the other foot, one of my remaining fingers and the thumb. Whirlwind, right? All in the space of four months.

I sat in my new hovel waiting to die. Waiting for important pieces to disappear. The parts that made me function. Maybe my mother was right. Maybe I was rotten.

My housing benefit barely covered a grotty studio. I needed a wheelchair by then and it was the only "accessible" place available.

It was damp, cramped, and my neighbours sold crack in the communal hallway. Confined by my body and my mind, I despaired. My entire, promising, young life had faded away month by month.

Halloween 2020 took my ears. Where the opening should have been were thin layers of smooth flesh and I stared at my broken reflection, raising my stump of a hand to the mirror, only my middle finger remaining.

It was torment. Worse than any of the other losses. I hadn't just lost the outer part; the entire ear canal was gone. I was entirely deaf.

It drove me to the brink of suicide. I couldn't bear the constant silence. So I acted. I took a knife and I stuck it deep into the fleshy voids where I knew my ears had been.

The pain was agonising, like my head was on fire. But it didn't work. No blood. No scars. They healed fucking instantly, and finally I accepted that I was dealing with something that wasn't medical. Something that wasn't a natural phenomenon at all.

My miserable world stayed silent. I laughed at the irony of wishing for magic so hard as a child. This was magic, wasn't it? I can't think of another explanation. Some sort of magic curse. Rotten.

November 5th made me realise that whatever was causing this was ramping it up. It made me realise that this was a one year only kind of deal. Both legs were gone. Both of them.

It wasn't just taking one piece anymore; it was making sure I wouldn't make it to next year.

Christmas came. Lockdown Christmas. I know. Everyone had it bad. I know. It wasn't a merry little Christmas; Santa clause did not come to town and all everyone wanted for it was some fresh air.

But did everyone wake up missing an arm? Ha. Just me? Thought so. Only one limb left and only one finger, too. I'd have struggled to open presents if I'd gotten any.

What a present. The last gift from this curse that's plagued me all year. Tomorrow is January 1st, 2021 and I don't expect that I'll wake up missing anything else. In fact, I just don't expect to wake up at all.

And that's where we are. New Year's Eve 2020 and it's really chipped away at me. I wish I could say I'm not scared to die but I am, it's petrifying, and I won't pretend otherwise.

The only silver lining, the only bright side to this curse is that I get to see the back of the year that took everything from me.

And it left me one single finger, just one, the one I'm typing this out with. I'll raise it tonight, to say fuck 2020.

INSANE IN THE MUNDANE

Mundane.

That's my life. Or it was. My life was an endless drawl of endless repetition. Work. Sleep. Eat. Repeat.

Have you ever had that feeling? The feeling that you're going nowhere. The sudden notion to up and leave everything you know and start afresh just for a single moment of excitement?

I have.

Every now and again something broke the cycle; a trip to a beautiful city and a chance to pretend I was someone I wasn't. A fuck, at the end of an intoxicated evening, without need for a more beautiful way of describing it.

Despite these dalliances, my life remained fundamentally the same.

Mundane.

I didn't anticipate that a travelling carnival, stopping in the next village over, would break that cycle.

Jolie took me. Her eyes lit up as she invited me to the circus, over the water cooler in our office. I didn't have the heart to tell her that a carnival and a circus weren't the same thing at all. I didn't have the heart to say no either.

She was a beautiful woman and a fantastic lover, I wished with every fibre of my being that I could muster more interest in her than my vested interest in her genitalia. I'm certain she hoped for the same. But it just wasn't there.

The lights and the stalls were entrancing. I'm not sure if it was the distraction they provided from my attractive companion's grating voice, or if there were a force I couldn't see, drawing me in.

I suppose that doesn't matter now.

We trudged from stall to stall, losing rigged games and succumbing to the will of the humble Carnie. Jolie stared at cheap stuffed toys with a longing in her eyes. I was starting to regret agreeing to attend at all; £30 down and not so much as a cuddle.

It was positively mundane.

As mundane as everything else in my life. I tried to take everything in with my eyes, but any attraction was obscured by vast swathes of people. Maybe I could slip into the crowd, disappear into obscurity, never see the office or Jolie again?

It was wishful thinking.

Towards the back of the seemingly infinite rows of games and goldfish, imprisoned in bags and bowls, we reached a small trailer. Only large enough for a few full-grown adults, its size was at odds with the grandiose claim painted in elaborate font on the side.

THE GREAT SPECULO. GLASS EATING MACHINE.

That was an exciting claim. Not mundane. It was one of those tricks I'd never been able to quite understand. How does a person chew and swallow glass?

A trick, right? Just a trick.

"That's not for me, let's try the ring toss one more time!"

Such a grating voice for such a beautiful woman. It sounded much better when she was moaning... much less like *actual moaning*.

I turned away from her pleading face and knocked on the trailer door. I heard the dramatic huff, but I ignored it. If there was one thing that might brighten my carnival experience, it was having the opportunity to work out how Speculo did it. How a person ate glass.

The door swung inwards with a sharp creek.

The great Speculo was a tall man, an imposing figure that wouldn't have been out of place displayed as the carnival "strong man." A smile crept across his face, turning upwards in the corners perfectly matching his styled moustache.

"You want to watch? Come in." He beckoned, and I followed.

Two steps. Two steps between the trailer door and the grass beneath. Two steps between me and something that wasn't mundane. Something exciting.

I sat opposite Speculo as Jolie hovered uncomfortably behind me. The small table only had space for one guest, and she was insistent she didn't want a front seat view to the show.

Between us was an array of clear, delicate glass items. A lightbulb, a snow globe and an empty bottle of vodka.

"Was the vodka to sterilise?" I asked, a wry grin on my face, thinking I had it all worked out.

Manipulated sugar sculptures. That was what I decided in the moment was the trick. I felt quite clever, as if I knew a secret about the man before me that no one else did. Like I'd outsmarted him.

"No." He replied. "It tastes better than the rest."

I sat back and prepared for the show. He smashed the bulb first, grabbed at a jagged shard and tossed it in his mouth, grinding it down with his teeth before swallowing, letting out a satisfied *"ahhhh."*

Then there was the globe. I watched the liquid pour as he shattered the casing on the table. Jolie shuddered behind me, I couldn't see it but I felt it, her discomfort permeated the air.

I sat back, smug, enjoying the convincing facade that Speculo had created. Watching as he lapped up every splinter of "glass."

"Is it sweet?" I asked, impressed by the craftsmanship of the faux items.

"It's delicious."

Finally, he smashed the bottle. Jolie jumped, causing the trailer to shake as the shards cascaded across the table, onto my lap and onto the floor. It was a beautiful sound, a symphony of crashing.

He tucked in, savouring every moment. I watched as he swished the bits of bottle around in his mouth, like a gorgeous wine that he wasn't ready to sacrifice to his stomach just yet. Had it been real glass it would've poked through the flesh of his cheeks for sure.

He wasn't even trying to keep up the facade anymore. It annoyed me. I came for a show, for something more than my mundane life, something *real*.

"Oh man, does that taste good?" I asked, noting his expression of ecstasy.

"The best." He responded.

That only annoyed me more. It was a lie. Speculo was a fraud and a phoney, and it incensed me enough that I felt the need to call him out. To prove it.

I picked up a large, sharp piece of the vodka bottle. It felt like glass in my hand, but I knew it was just an illusion. Or I thought I did.

I smiled as I threw it into my mouth and bit down hard, expecting an intense, sugary flavour, like a lollipop that had been intricately shaped. That wasn't what I got.

It took a moment.

Speculo laughed and Jolie screamed. Blood poured from the mouth as each ground edge embedded itself in my cheeks, my tongue, and forced its way down my throat.

I'd made a terrible mistake. A horrible, awful miscalculation. One that was going to cost me my life. What a way to die. An attempt to show up a professional sideshow freak wasn't how I'd expected I'd meet my end.

But at least it wasn't mundane.

THE LITTLEST SHEET GHOST

Halloween is the worst time of year for me.

I'm not scared of the pagan connotations, or the sheer capitalism of the thing. What terrifies me is what lurks beneath the masks and costumes that walk the streets that night.

The monsters that hide.

Ten years ago I lost my only son, Finley, on Halloween night. He was six years old, full of life, and desperate to dress as a pirate.

I stayed up all night on the eve of Halloween, sewing a toy parrot to the shoulder of his costume and fashioning a hat fit for Jack Sparrow himself. I'd have done anything for my sweet boy.

Finley's dad worked himself into a drunken stupor while I pricked holes in every finger for that damn parrot. I'd barely slept the next day, but as my beautiful child let out an *ARGH,* I was so proud. *Polly wants a cracker* he chirped, stroking the stuffed parrot.

When my friend Lisa offered to take him trick or treating, I was grateful. Our boys were friends, they lived on the same street, Finley would have a great time and I could get some well needed sleep. She came to collect him, her son dressed as a mummy, draped in yards of toilet roll.

I kissed Finley's forehead, sent my little pirate out the door and never saw him again.

Lisa said the boys were having a blast, they met three other, slightly older kids and joined them to knock at the next few houses. They were dressed as a mad scientist, a skeleton and a little sheet ghost. Lisa stood back in the street to give them some independence.

The other kids came running back from one garden but our boys didn't. Lisa went straight to the house, but the kids weren't by the door. She knocked, only to discover it was an elderly lady who had a sign asking for no trick or treaters.

She claimed she hadn't had any all night.

The three stranger children ran off before Lisa came out of the old woman's home, and beneath the costumes, no one the police spoke to knew who they were. The whole neighbourhood searched. Every door was knocked on. Every street combed.

And every trail ran cold.

I'd never felt pain like it. Visceral, throbbing pain within every part of my body. Years passed. The void in me never filled back up, a gaping wound left in my soul. Finley's dad drank himself to death days after the fourth Halloween without our son, and I was left alone.

That pain never got better. That loss. Every year on Halloween I sat at the door with a bowl of sweets waiting for Finley to knock. Waiting for him to come home.

I smiled through the tears as I handed lollipops to tiny monsters, none of them my own. Year in. Year out. Halloween bought nothing but misery, suffering and growth in that hollow feeling.

This year was different.

The tenth anniversary. It feels wrong to make something like my son's disappearance sound like such a celebratory event, but something about *ten years* felt poignant.

Like it was marking the loss of hope and a transition to mourning.

Finley would be sixteen. Too big to trick or treat, too obvious for any costume. Still, I filled that bowl and I sat at that door. And the little monsters came. Like every year before it.

I found it somewhat therapeutic. Watching kids with their parents; fairy princesses, mummy's, vampires, and even the occasional little pirate. Safe, happy. It sparked a burning jealousy but also an inexplicable joy. I'd always loved kids.

A single knock on my door changed everything.

I smiled in my chair as I listened to the knock, so low down on my door it could only have come from a child too small to reach the knocker. I expected a small gaggle, or a duo of creative costumes at least, but when I opened up the child was alone.

No friends. No parent standing a few metres behind. No *trick or treat.*

In front of me was what appeared to be a small, lost child, covered by a bedsheet with crude holes cut out for the eyes and mouth, black makeup smeared across the face beneath in a misguided attempt to elevate the costume.

I remembered sewing that parrot. Staying up all night.

This poor kid hadn't had more than 5 minutes spent on his costume. A little sheet ghost.

I thought back to the night that Finley disappeared. The moment that Lisa told me he was gone and described those other kids. I remembered their costumes. *The sheet ghost.* It was impossible, crazy in fact, but it still hurt to think that someone looking just like this may have been the last thing Finley saw.

"Hi! Would you like some sweets?" I asked softly, crouching to get closer to the child's level. Heart pounding. Something about the child... the costume... it made my heart race.

I realised quickly after my question that he wasn't carrying a sweet receptacle of any kind, no tiny pumpkin bucket nor plastic shopping bag. I couldn't see his hands at all under the sheet. No provision had been made for arm holes.

The child didn't say a word. The little ghost just stood stationary in the white sheet, looking back at me with dark, almost black eyes to match the bad makeup. I could've sworn they looked tearful. Lost.

"Are your parents nearby?"

BOO

That was all the little sheet ghost said. Just *BOO*, nothing else. Then he stood there, still. I took a step outside and looked up and down the street; surveying adults, all attached to small children, none looking for a little sheet ghost. The world had learned a lot in ten years.

Kids that small didn't wander freely anymore.

BOO

There was a pang in my stomach. A feeling I couldn't describe. What if this was what happened to Finley? What if he and his little friend knocked on the wrong door and were invited inside? *My sweet boy.* I wasn't going to do any harm, but the child should have been more cautious of strangers.

What if the next door the little sheet ghost knocked on *was* the wrong door?

"Do you want me to help you look for your parents?"

BOO

I didn't know what to do. My head was all over the place. It was like Finley was stood in front of me, under a tattered sheet, just out of reach. But it wasn't. I knew it wasn't. It was someone else's Finley. I surveyed the road again, but still couldn't see a single person out of place.

"What's your name?"

BOO

Every time I felt a train of reasonable thought it was interrupted by that sound. The Boo. The child's voice was dainty, soft, and ignited the maternal instinct in me that had stayed dormant for so long. Maybe that's why I did what I did.

Maybe that's why I took the child into my home.

BOO, the child responded when I offered to get them a glass of water. That was it. I thought I'd sit them down, call the police. Help someone not to go through what I did. Keep him warm and safe for his mum.

As the little sheet ghost crossed the threshold into my house, I realised the sheet dragged below where its feet would be. No arms visible, no feet visible either. The child was just an arch, the traditional badly drawn ghost shape.

A spectre of Halloween itself.

"Sit down if you like. I'm gonna make some calls and see if I can locate your parents."

The ghost didn't move, it didn't sit down. It just stood there. I tried to usher the child to the sofa, but at first they wouldn't move. And when they finally did, they overtook me in the hallway, before stopping still once more.

BOO, the little sheet ghost said as it stood stationary in front of me, blocking my path to the phone that I'd left on my kitchen table.

"Hey, buddy, please, just go sit down. I want to get you home safely."

For a few minutes, the little sheet ghost stood and looked at me, dark eyes welling with what looked like tears before I heard a sound I never expected to hear again. I was so transfixed on the eyes that it made me jump, more than any boo could.

Polly wants a cracker.

My heart dropped into the pit of my stomach. The voice didn't sound like the one that said *BOO*, it sounded just like my Finley.

"What did you say?" I asked, watching the little ghost much closer than I had been before. Wondering if my paranoia was getting to me. Wondering if this poor, lost child was triggering my pain so severely that I could hear my own son.

The little sheet ghost stood stationary. It didn't repeat what it said. Or Boo. But it didn't move either. I took a step towards it.

POLLY WANTS A CRACKER

The words were so loud. They weren't to be brushed off a second time. But the second time they weren't in my son's voice. The words were laden with violence, malice. Involuntarily, I clutched my hands to my ears. The little sheet ghost didn't move.

I knew it this time. The words. That phrase. It was the ghost. The kid. The little monster. Or was it? I didn't notice its mouth move at all. I realised I hadn't once seen it open, not for a single sound.

POLLY WANTS A FUCKING CRACKER

"Why are you doing this?" I sobbed. Looking at the unmoving, unconvincing spectre in front of me.

It just stood. Stupid, ghostly holes cut out of that sheet over its face, pulling outwards towards the bottom of the eyeholes. It infuriated me. Finley's story was public, was this some sort of cruel joke? The voice a recording, used to trick a grieving mother?

I felt the anger build up inside me, and I struggled to push it back down.

Instead, I pushed forwards, desperate to get past the little ghost, to get to my phone and call the police and end the nightmare. *This would be the last Halloween I sat by that door.* I would not be bullied by a child.

But that wasn't what happened.

The moment I made contact with that sheet I knew.

I knew *it* wasn't a child at all. The sheet folded inwards, meeting nothing solid. There was nothing beneath the sheet. No hidden feet. No hidden arms. It was the sheet. I stood back, now stationary myself, shock coursing through my veins.

BOO

The monster lurched forwards quickly, coming towards me with such velocity I didn't stand a chance. As it knocked me to the ground, I wrestled with handfuls of bedsheet, trying to unearth my tormentor. It was no use; the bedsheet wasn't bedsheet at all, just a part of the creature that had entered my home.

Pinning me to the ground, it came within inches of my face, floating like the spectre it was attempting to imitate, forcing me to clutch the floor for some sort of protection. Its size had no bearing on the terror I felt.

For the first time, its mouth opened. Its grotesque, blackened gums were lined with tiny, pointed teeth, like they'd been filed to be as dangerous as they possibly could be.

Polly wants a cracker it hissed, black saliva working its way around those teeth, dripping onto the white fabric-like material and onto my face, leaving a putrid scent in its wake.

"What did you do to my son?" I begged, tears streaming down my face as I realised that this absolutely was the last thing my son had seen. That it was never a child in a costume the first time. That the others probably weren't either.

The little sheet ghost laughed.

I couldn't bare the cruelty. Why had it come back for me now? What use was I to it?

ARGH ARGH ARGH ARGH

The ghost repeated my son's pirate noise, pitch perfect, like it had become that damn parrot on his shoulder. Mocking me, savouring my pain. I tried to scream, but I couldn't find the air. It went on for minutes. Minutes that felt like years.

Then it stopped.

The little sheet ghost stabilised. Returning to its stationary, childlike position. Starting at me in silence as I blubbered on the floor, a hysterical mess.

No. It said, off script for once, in the same soft and gentle voice that each evil *BOO* had come from.

"No, what?" I asked, the hollowness that I'd carried for years plugged with intense fear.

I don't want any sweets thank you, miss.

I was confused.

Miss, are you ok? Why are you on the ground?

Had I imagined the entire thing? Was this a real child in front of me? A real child that I'd imagined into a monster. Was I a monster? There was a fucking child in my home. Sitting up, my heart sunk even further than I thought possible as I noticed a pair of small feet in tattered old trainers.

A lost kid. A lost kid on Halloween and I'd scared the life out of him and then collapsed to the ground. I pushed myself back up to my feet and plastered a forced smile on my face.

"I'm... I'm sorry kid. I'm going to call the police, so they can find your parents."

I inhaled short, sharp breaths. Desperately trying to compose myself, but it never really mattered to begin with. Silently the little sheet ghost walked to the front door and turned to face me one last time.

I looked for them, but the trainers were gone, the spectral appearance back to what it once was.

The ghost opened his mouth, revealing the nightmarish teeth that I'd been unsure were real and simply stated, *no need,* before making awful retching sounds. Panic washed back over me as a green, fuzzy looking item, coated in black made its way out of the shrewdly cut mouth hole, landing on my floor.

I stared at it for a moment as the ghost stood in silence, smiling.

There it was. I couldn't ever forget it. The parrot. The same parrot I spent hours stitching to Finley's costume.

The little sheet ghost looked at me and licked its lips, savouring the pain on my face, and spoke through its grotesque teeth once more, before vanishing into nothingness.

I've tried to forget it happened, to convince myself that it was all a hallucination. A symptom of my grief. But every time I hold that parrot, I'm reminded it was real. And worst of all, I'm reminded of the little sheet ghost's last words.

I don't want any sweets, Miss. I already ate your sweet boy years ago.

THERE'S A NEFARIOUS CHICKEN ON MY LAWN

Yep.

You read that right. A chicken. A cockerel. A nefarious one. On my lawn.

Ridiculous. But let me take you back to the moment this started. The moment *Senior Cluck,* as I've not so lovingly nicknamed him, arrived on my property.

Three days ago. Usually not much happens to me in the space of three days, but these past few have changed my life, all because of that stupid, feathered fuck.

Well... I wish he were stupid.

I live in a suburb. *Little boxes, little boxes,* and not a single cow in sight. No farms or rural locations within at least 45 minutes. I liked it that way, never got stuck behind a tractor driving home. Yet still, as I opened my curtains that morning there he was.

Pecking at the grass. Prick. I'd sown fresh lawn seed only a week before.

I'm not sure what the appropriate reaction to a farmyard creature on your property is. So I took an approach often mocked when executed by elderly men like myself. I'm not sure what point in my life I lost the ability to deal with my issues, but I shook my fist at it. Yes. I shook my fist at it.

HEY, YOU CHICKEN... GET OFF MY LAWN!

I took a few steps outside, feeble and barely clenched fist in the air; Senior Cluck started to pay attention. He turned, just his head, not his body, and his beady eyes glowed red. He broke into a trot that became a sprint and leapt a few feet in the air, sharp looking toes coming at me.

I retreated. Shut the door and struggled to catch my breath. I hate getting old.

Three days ago, I'd have said I was embarrassed to have been intimidated by a chicken. But not now. Not anymore. This is a fucking warning.

I stood at the window until I convinced myself he would just go away. That I was wasting precious minutes of my life watching the pesky thing and that it was best I left to make breakfast. Without me watching, it might've wandered off. That was my logic. Wilfully forgetting the glow of the eyes.

Before I could even place my plate on the table by the window I was shaken by screams. Not just those of a single person, multiple. Dropping toast, jam side down, on the floor I rushed to the window.

Senior Cluck was in fully fledged battle chicken mode. He had gotten hold of my neighbour, Mrs. Darcy, and was savaging her.

Blood. Feathers. Clucking. It was clucking horrifically. No. That wasn't a typo, nor a pun; it's an unfortunately accurate representation of the scene outside my glass safety panel. I hesitated; did I rush outside? Call the police?

Call the police on a chicken. I couldn't fathom that, so I opened the door again, this time picking up my cane in the hallway. I rushed towards the woman but I couldn't get anyway near. Senior Cluck wasn't alone, and three more birds attacked, forcing me to flee back inside.

Eventually, Mrs. Darcy stopped screaming. She collapsed to the ground and hit the cement with her face, while her feet remained on my blood-spattered lawn. Senior Cluck lifted his beak to the sky and let out a bloodcurdling war cry, his accomplices pecking near his feet.

COCK-A-DOODLE-DOO

I gasped, it took a moment before I realised that the other screaming I'd heard, the different human voices… they hadn't stopped. I'd barely seen a thing but feathers in my venture outdoors, so I pressed my face to the glass, peering up and down the road to see sights beyond my worst nightmares.

Every house had a chicken.

Hens. Cockerels. Fluffy, ornamental and smooth. They stretched as far as I could see, and so did the bodies. Unsuspecting neighbours. Mostly the young who had thought they could easily remove a chicken from their lawn.

Wouldn't you? Wouldn't you go and move the chicken? Well, you'd have fucking died.

They all died.

One by one I watched the people slump to the ground and the birds screech victorious into the sky. The usually quiet street was ironically alive, a cacophony of distressing sounds running straight through me.

I tried to dial the police... ambulance... anyone who would come, but my landline wasn't working, looking outside I noticed the telephone line that ran just behind the houses opposite had been severed.

As the last person, a young lad down the street who'd driven an obnoxiously loud car in life lost his valiant battle, the chickens stopped in unison.

A deadly silence.

The sky greyed, despite the sun having just risen and slowly they all stepped towards their victims. Heads bobbing furiously, each of them took position on their individual podiums.

It's a sight I never expected to even consider. An entire road full of corpses, each with its poultry murderer stood proud on top. Senior Cluck turned his head an entire 180 degrees and glared through the window at me, feet planted on Mrs. Darcy's chest.

I spent hours at that window. The day went by. His head never turned back around to face the same direction as his body. He was watching. He spent the whole day watching.

I watch back.

The second day there was a resistance. The loved ones of the dead headed outside, in a much more organised fashion. Weapons of all descriptions were strewn across the street. The rebels managed to claim a few of the birds, but whenever one died another appeared.

They didn't stand a chance.

Senior Cluck, the obvious pack leader, didn't move from the rotting corpse of Mrs. Darcy. He didn't partake in the war, but he had control. He commanded his troops from position, squawking and crowing with sounds I can only describe as angry.

He never turned his head either, he continued to watch me. I shut the curtains, tried just peeking through from the top, but he was still facing the house. Always. He understood exactly what I was thinking, planning.

I didn't stand a chance either. I didn't even try.

This morning I woke on my chair by the window. For a single, beautiful second I thought it had all been a dream, but I was reminded of my cruel reality by Senior Clucks evil face, mere centimetres from mine, just the pane of glass to separate us.

He's been there all day, eyes glowing a furious red. The others are back on their dead podiums, some turned to face their respective houses. My theory is that the ones whose heads are turned have survivors in the houses.

The sky never changed from the miserable grey. The police never came.

They must have been called, I've got to be the only miserable old fucker with a landline and no mobile. Someone had to have called them. It didn't make sense to have this many bodies and no police. Fuck, I'd have taken military tanks and a glass dome over the neighbourhood at this point. I've never wanted police near me this badly, but I don't think they're going to come.

Maybe they died too.

Maybe this problem is a lot more widespread than it first seemed. Do you have a chicken on your lawn?

I don't know what to say. Senior Cluck is still at the window. He's watching me and I've worked out what he wants... it's in the eyes. The Beady, glowing eyes.

He wants the world.

THE STORY OF APRIL STRANGE

April Strange was born with half a face.

No matter what iteration of the story you heard, or how many details differed from the last, it always started the same. With a sad little girl missing half her face.

April Strange was a well-known legend in the village. She was the daughter of the mayor in the early 1900s and she disappeared aged only nine years old.

That much was fact. April Strange had a tragic existence, and her vanishing act only resulted in more conspiracies surrounding the ill-fated girl. A small village like ours loves to gossip.

It was said that April was badly bullied at school. Her father opted to send her to a local, public school despite his vast wealth. He wanted her to be a grounded child, with roots in her community.

Mayor Strange didn't listen to her complaints about class or how she was teased by the other children. He saw her merely as an accessory; his poor, disfigured daughter who could win him the sympathy vote and improve public perception.

That's all speculation of course. It's a story that has been passed down for generations. Edited to fit whoever was listening to the tale. I'll continue with the version I was told. The one that haunted my whole childhood.

April's bullying took a nasty turn. She wore her hair long and over her face, which only attracted the attention of the bullies as it wasn't in keeping with the times. During a craft session at school a particularly vile boy named Edwin Mode crept up behind April and grabbed hold of her long locks before severing them with scissors.

April Strange cried, and the class sat and laughed, mocking the dejected girl. Their attacks intensified and soon they were following her home regularly, calling her awful names, tripping her up and trying to push her into puddles.

No one is really sure what happened to April. She left her house one morning and never arrived on the school bus; there was a well-documented investigation that turned up absolutely nothing.

The most commonly accepted theory is that the bullies took things too far one day and killed the girl before conspiring to bury their mistake. Several kids were late for school the day of the disappearance and they were reported as "acting shifty" but not a shred of evidence was found. And not one of them broke.

Until Edwin Mode broke.

Not as in broke down and told the police what happened to April. No. The village kids had formed some sort of pact and none of them were going to confess to the murder.

Edwin Mode quite literally broke in two. He was climbing a tree on the green with friends and made it higher than he ever had before. He raised his arms in victory and the branch broke, sending Edwin plummeting. After a particularly nasty drop, he landed on a strong upright branch that split his entire body down the middle. It was a grisly sight.

The town mourned. I remember my older sister telling me the story for the first time and pulling out old newspapers that my great grandmother had collected. Articles outlining the tragedy of a minute village that had lost two children in the space of a few weeks.

It was tragic, but that's all it was. The death of Sally Greenwood was what turned April Strange into a local campfire legend.

Sally Greenwood was a known bully. There were witnesses to her tormenting April, and she was a good friend of Edwin. Devastated by the news of his death, Sally visited the small playground by the village hall to play on the swing set, like she and Edwin had before his untimely demise.

As she swung morosely a screw at the top of the swing set's large metal frame loosened. Sally was too sad to notice. A local teen walking his dog saw her swinging. He also saw the frame collapse, instantly crushing Sally Greenwood's head into mush.

My sister told me that he got her brains on his shoes. I'm not sure if that's true. But it terrified me as a child.

The teen spoke to the police and reported seeing two girls, one swinging and one climbing the frame, who weren't there after the accident. He described the other girl, matching April Strange's description to the letter.

Another failed manhunt ensued, and speculation over the two freak accidents sparked widespread hysteria. The villagers believed that the ghost of April Strange was seeking vengeance on the kids that wronged her. And not a single one of them had enough faith in their child's innocence to believe they were exempt.

What a sad indictment on attitudes to children in those days. Was it a wonder that they were so cruel to April? Their parents had been too complacent to teach them empathy.

The mass panic became such a source of distress for Mayor Strange and his wife that they shut down the search for their daughter.

A string of unexplained and grotesque accidents plagued the village children. They died indiscriminately, each in a more horrifying fashion than the last. Many witnesses to these unfortunate accidents insisted they had seen a young girl with only half a face.

The parents of the dead kids never talked about April. Some folk speculated that they were trying to ignore the truth, others speculated that April Strange herself visited them, blaming them for the deaths and condemning them to a life filled with guilt.

Many of the mothers and fathers committed suicide or spent time in insane asylums. I suppose that's to be expected when one loses their child so young and with so little purpose.

Almost an entire class of children were wiped out. A few remained. Those who had often been targets of the bullies themselves or who had shown April what small kindness she knew in her short life.

They passed the story down to their children, who passed it onto their children. The tale was largely used as a tool to convince kids to be nice to each other.

Adults tried to play it down to any child that was too scared. But they couldn't deny the pattern of problem children found dead in outlandish accidents. And they couldn't hide that from their own children. For a tiny population, the village's mortality rate was through the roof.

I remember the nightmares I had as a kid, images of April Strange staring with her one eye through my windows plagued my dreams. It was a story far too frightening for the children it was told to, but for the most part, it worked.

I never made fun of another kid. I know many of you will think that I'm lying, but I really never did. I was far too scared of the girl with half a face coming to get me to even consider it. And so were most of the village children.

As I got older, I didn't think about April as much. During high school I would've laughed at anyone taking the urban legend seriously. She occasionally made her way into my thoughts at poignant moments; once when a new girl joined my class and I felt compelled to be her friend and make sure that everyone was nice to her.

Another time April crossed my mind was when that same girl's younger brother was found face down in a pool of blood in the primary school bathroom. He had slipped on soap that had been dripped when some kids, who had been in the bathroom just moment before him, used it to stick toilet paper to the ceiling.

He was propelled forwards, hitting the sink with such force that he gave himself a fatal head injury. By chance no one entered the bathroom for around 30 minutes, leaving him to die on the floor.

He didn't know the story of April Strange. He had called a girl ugly just an hour before he died, making her cry in front of her peers. Village people gossiped about the ghost, just like they had all those years ago.

I couldn't deny the striking coincidences that made the tale so terrifying. My new friend moved away not long after. Her parents had heard enough tales of a hundred-year-old dead girl to think that we were all batshit crazy. That's what I presumed anyway. I didn't take proper note of the haunted expression that they both wore, that held more fear than it did grief.

I couldn't blame them for leaving.

Years passed without incident. The story had been shared so widely that our town became quite a friendly place for young children. Kids can be cruel, but kids behave when there's fear involved. They all knew someone who had succumbed to the supposed curse. It was enough to keep them in line.

I married a local man not long after high school and we moved into a modest sized home. I worked as a night carer and he as a fisherman. A few years after our wedding I gave birth to a beautiful baby boy. We named him Henry, and he was perfect.

I doted on my son, throwing myself into motherhood with everything I had. In truth, I probably spoiled him a little. He was a jealous baby, who didn't want to share toys at playgroup. I tried desperately to teach him kindness and tolerance, but my life became a cacophony of other mothers tutting in disapproval.

I thought of April and vowed that I would tell him the tale when he was old enough to understand. I wasn't certain of the story's truth myself, but I wasn't willing to take the risk.

As Henry grew, he was as sweet as sugar whenever his father and I were watching. Our concerns from his pre communicative phase appeared unfounded. My son had lots of friends and, once he reached preschool, glowing reviews from his teachers.

There never seemed to be an appropriate time to sit Henry down and discuss the story of April Strange with him. It just never came up. What point should a parent deem it necessary to terrify their child like that?

I remember a friend bringing their son over for a play date and she had just told him the story after catching him harassing her very unsociable cat. The poor kid was traumatised. She said he hadn't slept all night and he looked as if part of his innocence had been ripped away from him. It seemed too harsh a punishment. Too harsh a way to teach a lesson. I couldn't in good faith do that to Henry.

After all, I couldn't see that I had anything to worry about. My son was a good boy, he was no bully.

In Henry's third year of school, I was proven wrong. I was called in at pickup time to discuss an incident with his teacher.

My son had taken a girl's glasses and held them out of reach, eventually dropping them resulting in smashed glass and a very visually impaired child. His teacher was sombre as she told me, she knew exactly what Henry's actions meant.

I hadn't told him the story. And I was going to suffer for it.

I was horrified at my son's behaviour. I lambasted him, but I also didn't let him out of my sight. I must have watched his reflection in the rear-view mirror more than the road as we drove home.

I saw potential catastrophe everywhere. So I came up with the bright idea to build a pillow fort in the living room. Henry loved forts. I knew I shouldn't be rewarding him for his bad behaviour, but the pillows seemed to be the safest option. I could stay in it with him and even if it collapsed, he would be safe.

I cursed myself silently. *Ridiculous.* I thought to myself as I processed spending my time and energy protecting myself from a ghost story invented to scare children.

Still, I couldn't shake the images of April in my mind. The sad little dead girl with half a face.

I tried to keep my eyes open all night. I didn't leave his side. His father was out working for the night so I couldn't share my burden, I was left alone to deal with my anxieties. But I couldn't deter bodily functions.

Around 11pm I had to pee. I'd tried to hold it for so long, but I couldn't do it any longer. Henry was asleep. He couldn't have been in a safer position than he was. Two minutes couldn't hurt, surely?

I sat in the brightly lit bathroom upstairs in our home. Thinking of the mistakes I'd made. Wondering if it was too late to tell my son the story, to save him from his own cruelty. Then the knocking came.

tap... tap... tap!

It was slow and calculated, not the result of a bird or tree branch. And it was coming from outside the upstairs bathroom window. My blood ran cold. I picked up my knickers and peered through the gap in the open top section.

What I saw nearly caused a heart attack.

A great mass of maimed and contorted children, forming a spectacularly macabre ladder of sorts, directly to the window. I tried to move my legs, to run down the stairs to my son, but I couldn't. I was frozen to the spot, taking in the morbid pile of flesh.

I suddenly understood why none of the dead kid's parents had chosen to speak about the accidents. How could they even begin to explain *this?*

A small figure worked its way up the chain. It reminded me of the masses that ants form in order to float or climb. The entire structure moved and adapted, bones and limbs extending to form pegs for the climbing child. Parts of bodies writhed in sickening motion.

When she reached the top, she looked me dead in the eyes. She was everything I had imagined, the exact face that had haunted my childhood nightmares for years. And I was face to face with her.

April Strange.

Her lone eye was filled with sadness, tears glazing its surface and highlighting the brilliant blue colour of her iris. The missing half of her face wasn't scarred, like you would expect in someone with a disfigurement like hers. The skin was smooth, like the features were never supposed to be there in the first place.

We stared at each other for a lingering moment. She was so mesmerising I was briefly distracted from the horrendous human tower that she balanced on top of. Only briefly.

In my peripheral vision I noticed a boy, his face staring up at me from around halfway up the ladder. His mouth was wide open with a large, thick tree branch jutting out of it. Edwin Mode. April was balancing on the bodies of her own victims.

She noticed the shock in my eyes and I noticed the sadness in hers developing into anger and malice. She opened her mouth, fused together on one side, and in a raspy, obviously unused voice, she spoke.

You should have taught him to be nice. This is all your fault.

Her words were accompanied by an almighty crash from downstairs and a half smile, stretched across the side of her face. I felt my heart thumping against my rib cage as I pondered what fate my son may have met.

In a blink, she was gone. Along with the whole monstrous structure that she arrived on. I took a sharp inhale and forced my weak legs to turn and bolt down the stairs.

I was too late.

There's no worse feeling than the anticipation of something awful. Especially when that particular something is inevitable. As I turned the doorknob to enter the front room, I prepared for the horrors that I might face. Preparation didn't make me feel ready though. Nothing could've readied me for what I saw.

The dusty old feature light that hung in the centre of the ceiling had snapped from its fixture. The faux crystals and beads scattered the floor... some spattered with crimson flecks.

I wept as I spotted the damp red pillow that had once been a brilliant white, with a piece of metal leaf detailing from the light speared through it. Fighting tears and the urge to vomit, I moved the pillow aside to finally reveal my son.

Henry had been impaled through the head deep enough to penetrate his brain. There was no way to save him. The long, narrow piece of metal had destroyed his beautiful face.

Well. Half of it.

April had made sure that whenever I thought of my son, this image would be burned into my mind. Her image.

I wish things could've been different. I wish I hadn't been so concerned with scaring him. Now I spend my days riddled with guilt, imagining how painful eternal damnation to the ghost girl's tower must be.

I wish I had just told him the story of April Strange.

RUN

Ever wanted to run away? Hide for a few minutes? Lock yourself in the bathroom at work just to avoid the deathly glare of your desk? Maybe fake your own death and escape to a beach in Bali.

I have. And I did.

I ran. I can't pinpoint the exact moment I made the decision; there was no one traumatic moment or dramatic escapade forcing me underground.

To really simplify the situation, I just hated my life.

I worked a dead-end job, had few friends and no partner. My parents died when I was young, and I was left with no siblings. My folks were alcoholics, and if any extended family existed, then they certainly never knew that I did.

I worked ridiculous hours just to struggle to pay my rent at the end of the month and when I really thought about it, I didn't have a single prospect. I drank too, not as bad as my parents but I did, sneaking the occasional shop brand vodka into my bag without paying during a food shop.

Sounds bleak, right?

Well, it was. It was fucking bleak, and I hated every moment of it.

So I packed a bag.

Just one. Not even a backpack or a suitcase; just a large handbag with a few hygiene essentials and a few changes of underwear. I went to the bank and closed my account, emptying it of all cash; a grand total of £897. Woefully under-prepared, I filled my car with fuel and hit the road.

I had no aim and no real intention. I wanted to cross the channel, maybe travel through Europe and start a new life in Florence, or maybe Amsterdam. Unfortunately, I never made it that far.

After about an hour of driving and five or six calls from my employer, I threw my phone out the window and my nightmare truly began.

I should've checked the rear-view mirror first. I should've looked to see how close the car behind me was, but I didn't. The mixture of speed and wind carried the phone just far enough to smash through the front window, causing the driver to veer into the dividing wall between the two directions of fast paced traffic.

There was a multi car pileup and eventually, a fire. I managed to catch that in my rear-view mirror.

I didn't stop. I'm not proud of it but I didn't. I'm even less proud of the feeling of relief I experienced knowing that my phone would melt in the fire. I thought that meant I was free. That any evidence of me of the horrific thing I'd just done was gone and I would make it.

12 people died in that accident.

I know this because it took the police practically no time at all to find my vehicle, that's numberplate had been picked up by multiple traffic cameras. They found me attempting to sleep in the backseat, shivering in an industrial estate.

The concrete slab in the cell I spent the night in wasn't much warmer. I wondered if prison would really be any worse than the misery that I was already running from, or if the guilt of the accident would drive me slowly insane. There was a pain in my head and a sinking feeling in my stomach unlike anything I'd ever experienced.

I got no peace or sleep that night.

The next morning, I waited for something to happen. I expected more police, or a station staffer to come and process me, or something... *anything*. I'd had no food or fluids and I was certain someone would have to at least tell me what was going to come next. But they never did.

It took me a while to realise how remarkably quiet the station was, and how I had seen no one pass my cell for a number of hours. All the noise in my head had been so distracting.

Panic crept over my whole being as hours passed. I'd wanted a quiet life. I'd wanted to get away. But not like this.

The day passed and the slither of outside light that I could see through the slot in the cell door disappeared. Not a single human visited or spoke in, and I felt myself start to grow desperate as time progressed. I screamed. I screamed out for help or attention of any kind, but nobody came.

My throat burned after a while, after hours of desperate crying and yelping. I was so tired my eyelids had grown heavy and back against the door, I passed out from exhaustion.

I awoke to the slither of light, just touching the very tip of the opposite wall. Back seized and eyes swollen from tears, I gasped, as I noticed a man sitting on the concrete slab of a bed.

He was dressed in a suit, smart and well-tailored to his body. An older gentleman, with wrinkles creating abstract patterns on his face, he retained a level of attractiveness unusual for his age.

"Hello." He boomed, voice deep and commanding.

"Who are you?" I asked, shuffling up the wall into a standing position, fighting the pain of my seized limbs.

"Does it matter? You wanted to be nameless and I'm going to respect that. I think I'm going to remain nameless too."

"What is this place?"

"This is a police station, and you're sitting in a cell. Tell me... is this where you wanted to be?"

I shook my head.

"I didn't think so. Beach in Bali, was it?" The man squinted and leaned forward, edging closer to me. "Ohhh... it was a European road trip. Well. Good job you didn't make it much further after that road safety incident, isn't it? But of vodka to steel your nerves before the trip?"

"What do you want from me?" I cringed, thinking of the half empty bottle the police had no doubt found in my car.

"You ask far too many questions. None of this is about me. It's about you. The... woman... who... ran." He hissed the last words, taking time to pause and lift himself into a standing position, stepping towards me.

"I never meant to hurt anyone. I just... couldn't do it anymore."

"That's more like it. But you did hurt people... oh boy, you hurt a lot of people."

The man sinisterly smiled, and figures began to appear around him. I clutched the wall, trying to remain as far from them as possible as I counted 12 in total, including a woman clutching a baby with one arm and holding a toddler's hand with the other.

I knew who they were. I knew exactly why they were there. I fought the urge to vomit.

"I'm so sorry." I sobbed, struggling to find an adequate way to quantify my guilt.

In an instant they all disappeared, leaving just the well-dressed man behind.

"Sorry means nothing. They're dead, they can't hear you. I just wanted you to see what you'd done. To really feel it. Before I offer you a chance to decide again."

I frowned, eyes blurred and head pounding.

"What do you mean... decide again?"

"Finally, a question worth asking." He cackled, savouring my fear. "I can let you go back. I can let you try to change your own life rather than trying to make up a new one. I can give you the opportunity to give all those people their lives back, but you have to agree to my condition."

"Please, anything."

"You can't run again. This is your do over. You don't get another one.... Easy right? *Poof* everyone's happy."

"Of course. I'll do it. I promise... please let me go back."

The man smiled again, sending a shiver down my spine.

I knew I could keep that promise. Why would I ever try to run after what I'd seen and been through? I'm not a monster.

I don't recall the transition. I didn't fall asleep or wake up or see sparkles and lights. I just suddenly wasn't there anymore. The dingy cell was gone, replaced with my own living room.

It took a few days to recover from the shock. I called in sick at work, assuring them I'd be back. I cleaned my house, caught up on sleep and ordered pizzas to satiate the hunger that had grown in the cell, my last reminder that it even happened at all.

I searched the internet for details of a crash, but there was no record. The date had even changed, back to the day before I ran.

Weeks passed. I returned to my mundane routine, rediscovering the reasons I'd hated it so much in the first place. I wondered if I'd have been better off in that cell, but every time a thought like that crossed my mind, I imagined the figure of the mother and her children.

I tried. I tried so hard to continue.

Weeks turned into months and with that, life became hard to bear once more. I started drinking a lot. Thoughts of running crossed my mind again and I often found myself wondering what would happen if I broke the agreement.

Would I be transported back to that cell? Would exactly the same thing happen, and would all those people die again?

I weighed up every factor. I thought about every possible outcome.

And I ran my phone over in the driveway before I left.

I know. I know how selfish and egotistical I sound. But have you ever felt so desperate to escape from a suffocating existence that you'd go to any lengths to do so? Have you ever felt like that every single day?

I hit the road one more time. Terrified, I worried that somehow the man would know what I'd done, and I'd be plucked from the driver's seat and transported into whatever realm that frozen cell existed in.

That would've been preferable, I'm sure.

Instead, he waited to come for me. He waited until my breaks had already failed in the middle of a busy bottleneck, caused by an earlier accident. He waited until after my vehicle had careened into the one in front, causing a pile up that made the previous one look positively benign. He waited until after I'd noticed the mother and her two children burning in the car next to mine.

Then finally, as my face was melting in the flames, he came.

He sat next to me in the car, remaining miraculously untouched by the dirty yellow flames ripping through my body. He spoke only briefly, before leaving me to my fate.

"If only you'd realised that what you had was as good as it was ever going to get."

MY LAST PASSENGER WAS A NIGHTMARE

When I met my wife, it was like everything in the world made sense all at once. She was truly beautiful. Long, wavy auburn hair cascaded down her shoulders, throwing out tones of bright ginger and blonde in the sunlight. Her eyes were a striking green and flicked upwards in the corner like a natural cat eye.

Stunned didn't even begin to cover my feelings when I first saw her. I was a stuttering mess on our first date, but somehow, this angelic woman wanted to see me again. Our relationship blossomed, but I never stopped worshiping her. I was in awe of everything about her, from that silky gorgeous hair to her personality, that I had discovered perfectly complemented mine.

We got married young and had two children together, a little girl named Freya and a son named Frankie. My family were my whole world, everything I did was for them.

I worked hard as an overnight taxi driver to provide for my wife and kids. I hated every minute of it. Nights came with lots of drunk and rude people. Although we were allowed to charge more at that time, it didn't make up for the extra shit we had to put up with compared to the day drivers. It was awful, but worth it for the look on my kids' faces every time they got a present or we took them away for a week.

Around 6 months ago my life changed forever due to an incident with a passenger in my taxi.

She was young, maybe 16 to 18, and looked like she'd done a lot of drugs. Her eyes were sunken back into her skull and sat above deep, black bags. Her blonde damaged hair was ratty and broken, leading from a set of greasy, dark roots. She bit her nails throughout the entire ride, even for the brief moments we spoke they didn't leave her mouth. In my rear-view mirror, I could see the feint outline of blood surrounding them as she gnawed at them.

Being a driver that worked the graveyard shift, people in bad states were nothing new to me. Sadly, even young girls like this one were common. I knew the moment that she entered my car that she wasn't going to pay.

Usually, when I pick up a fare like this, I'll ask for the money upfront, but I felt so sorry for this young girl that I didn't. I figured if she ran out on me maybe I'd at least have got her somewhere she felt safe. She shook as if she was cold in the back the entire time, chewing on her nails like she was desperate to separate them from her fingers.

When we reached her destination, we pulled up outside some awful looking flats, cracked windows in the building and broken bottles on the ground outside. There was a chain fenced building site a few doors down the road that's fencing had been bent to allow people into the site, squatters I presumed.

As I anticipated, the girl panicked when I asked her for the £6.90 fare. She looked at me in the rear-view mirror with sheer terror in her eyes and unbuttoned her sheer blouse, revealing a painfully thin frame and a myriad of bruises all over her.

I told her to stop. That I wasn't interested, asked her to give me her name and let me take her somewhere safer. She said no to all of it. Despite her protests, she didn't get out of the car. I thought there might be some kind of hope for helping her out of her situation, maybe she really did want help but just didn't know how to ask.

I was preparing myself to manually lock the doors and drive the girl to the police station when I saw a large, tall figure emerge from the flats we were parked by.

The man came charging up to the car just as the manual locks clicked and hammered on the windows. The girl in the back now hysterical, begging to be let out. My act of attempted chivalry had seriously backfired.

The man's huge fists pounded on my passenger window so hard I was sure they would cave in. The girl had prized the lock open from the back and got out to hide behind this huge, intimidating figure. Blouse still unbuttoned.

As soon as she closed the door, I revved up the engine to drive away, locking the doors manually one more time. As I drove away, he shouted that I was a creep and a pervert. But catching last glimpses of the girl I felt like my instincts to try to get her to safety had been right.

As a taxi driver, I'm used to passengers running without payment, or having altercations in the dead of night when I'd rather be at home cuddling my wife. This girl and her big boyfriend were nothing new, unfortunately. It was a sad indictment of the reality we live in, but nothing new.

What was new to me, was the phone call I received the next day from the control room who allocate our jobs. They called to tell me about a complaint that had been made about me trying to kidnap and assault a young, vulnerable female. It had been called in by an incredibly rude, angry man threatening to take things further. The lady from control, Susan, was a good woman, who I often bantered with in the office. She knew me well, even attending Freya's recent birthday party.

So it was especially heart breaking when she delivered the news that although the company would not be contacting the authorities, they would have no choice but to take me off the books with no reference for any future companies I tried to sign up with.

One passenger. Someone I was trying to help, and suddenly I was jobless, unable to provide for my family.

When I received the news, all I could think of was my beautiful wife. I couldn't bear to see the disappointment in her bright, green eyes. The panic that we would no longer be able to give Frankie and Freya the lives we wanted them to have. I imagined having to explain why it had happened.

So I didn't tell her.

I knew it was wrong. But I just couldn't do it. I left in the car every night at 8pm just like I always had. Drove aimlessly around our local town and the neighbouring few, stopping at car parks looking for work online and in papers. I figured if I could get a job quick enough, she would never need to know.

One night, around 3 weeks into my unemployment, I was sat in the car park of a local supermarket, with a reading lamp and a newspaper, circling jobs that looked interesting and wouldn't require a reference from my previous employer. Pickings were slim. I flipped a few pages and came across an incredibly disturbing article.

Pictured was a young girl. The same young girl I'd picked up in my taxi those weeks ago. She looked healthier in the photo, her cheeks were fuller, and the black bags underneath her eyes were gone. She looked like a normal teenage girl. Next to the healthy-looking photo was another photograph of her back, covered in huge purple welts and bruises.

The article was describing her death. At the hands of a drug dealer who had been suspected of trafficking girls anyway. He had been caught driving under the influence with 1000s of pounds worth of narcotics in his car. And she, of course, beaten and bloodied in the boot. I recognised his photograph immediately as the large, intimidating man.

I sobbed into my steering wheel. Why hadn't I done more? Why hadn't I called the police? Why didn't I put up more of a fight with Susan? So many questions ran through my mind. I felt responsible for the death of this fragile little girl.

I'm ashamed to say that I didn't handle the news in the best way. It didn't inspire me to go home and tell my wife about my job. Or to take responsibility and get a new job quicker to help my situation. Instead, it drove me to the bottle.

My downfall was ugly. I would spend hours in car parks getting utterly wasted in the dead of the night. I'm humiliated by my actions. I drove drunk and didn't care about my own life or consider the danger I presented to others. I went home with brutal hangovers, unable to spend any quality time with my family, and spent time drinking in the day when I thought no one could see.

My addiction went hand in hand with a lack of sleep. Every time I closed my eyes all I saw was that scared little girl chewing on her nails so hard they bled. My wife and I argued constantly, but I never opened up to her.

Despite my abject stupidity, I was intelligent enough to understand the risks of drinking in my vehicle in public car parks in the open. Even in the pitch black of night. So I found more secluded spots, lay-bys and building sites became my friends, until I eventually found the perfect place to hide from my responsibilities.

It was a set of 3 parking spaces, at the mouth of a large park that doubled as a forest complete with camping site. In the daytime it was favoured as a dog park and space for creating family memories. In the night, it was my haven from the shame and hurt I was feeling and somewhere to keep up my lies.

The first night I made it through an entire bottle of vodka just sitting in the driver's seat of my car, staring into the wooded area directly in front of my car. It was completely still, even the birds were sleeping. The quiet bought some comfort to the torture my mind had been going through.

I soon started driving to that spot nightly. I would leave at 8pm and hit a few of my usual supermarkets to but supplies for the night before heading to the spot as darkness fell.

There was never another car in the car park. I saw the occasional group of teenagers trying to smoke weed in the dark but other than that I was always left alone. I frequented that spot for an entire month until I first saw it.

In that month my wife and I had begun to argue nonstop. My drinking had become a problem in the family home, and she couldn't understand why I was earning so little. I still couldn't find the courage to tell her I was slowly squandering our life savings on my addiction and lies. We argued badly before I left that night.

I put it down to lack of sleep and booze that first time. When she appeared, standing there covered in bruises. She wore the same sheer blouse that she had when I picked her up. Unbuttoned still. With tiny denim shorts showing off her long, thin, purple legs. She stood there amongst the trees just starting at my car. Not really moving, other than to ferociously bite at what little fingernail appeared to be left on her bloody digits.

Her sunken, blackened eyes were back. Burrowing deep into my soul with every second that we kept eye contact. I couldn't bear to look, but it was also impossible to look away. I must have sat there for at least an hour, swaying. Everything moved and spun a little, in that boozy vision that was becoming my norm. Everything, that is, except her.

She stayed entirely steady. Just staring at me, the world tilting around her as she remained still, aside from the incessant chewing.

I didn't sleep that night at all. Maybe that contributed to me returning the next night, I suppose people make poor decisions when they don't sleep. Or maybe my mind was just shot to pieces from the booze anyway. Either way, I returned. Either way, she was there again.

She looked slightly more battered than she had the night before, bruises had turned deeper shades of purple and her eyes seemed to have sunk further than possible for a living human. The flesh covering her bony frame was papery and transparent in the areas that weren't beaten. She had moved slightly closer to the car, just a few steps, but enough that even in my drunken state I had noticed, and it unnerved me.

I drove away early that night, I even came home early. Telling my wife, as she stirred when I came in, that it had been a slow night and I decided to come home. I suspected she smelled the alcohol on my breath, but she didn't say a word, just made a soft noise of acknowledgement.

I found some comfort in listening to her breathe that night. Watching the rhythmic rise and fall of her chest offered a distraction to the images of that young, dead girl that plagued my mind. I laid in bed, watching. It took until the morning for me to notice that I had bitten my nails until they bled, leaving exposed nail bed on several.

The following night I drove out like I always do. I avoided my spot; I couldn't face seeing her anymore. It wasn't healthy for me; my mind was playing all sorts of tricks on me and my heavy drinking was contributing to serious issues in my mind. My nails were excruciatingly sore as they pressed against my steering wheel.

I burned through so much gas that night, just driving around, but I didn't see her. Not standing in front of me anyway, nothing could remove her image from my mind. Her eyes begged for help.

After a few nights I realised that I couldn't sustain the petrol I was burning without picking up fares. I needed somewhere to stop if I was going to keep up my lies. I racked my brains, that were frazzled from a full week of sleep deprivation and whiskey.

I drove back there. I can see the error of my decisions now, but at the time I was blinded by the alcohol I was drowning in. Something kept drawing me back there. I wish it hadn't, but it did.

She was there, waiting for me.

This time she had become a literal corpse, there were no visible signs of breathing or life left in her, that tattered sheer blouse still hung unbuttoned, revealing ribs that resembled a child's drawing of ocean waves, the blues and greens that would make up an ocean in the picture just adding to layers of bruises in this ghastly scene.

She came closer than ever before. Her bloodied, stubby fingers tapped on my car bonnet, sending shivers through my whole body with every tap. I closed my eyes, scrunching up my face and willing her to go away. When I opened my eyes, she had.

My joy was short lived, she had disappeared from in front of my car, but as my eyes strayed towards the rear view mirror I saw her sunken eyes, staring back at me from the same seat she had sat in the first time I picked her up. When she was alive.

I screamed and scrambled out of the car, emptying my stomach contents on the hard, leafy ground as I exited the vehicle. My hands rested on my knees as I bent over, trying to stop myself from throwing up again. It took a while to stand up and steady myself, but when I did she was gone again. She wasn't in front of or inside my car.

I was about to get back in and drive home. I was going to confess everything to my wife, ask for help. I was losing my mind and I needed to do something about it, I couldn't go on like this. Then I glimpsed something out of the corner of my eye, something hanging trapped between the closed gap in the boot.

I moved closer to the back of the car, the sickness creeping back up in my stomach as I approach my closed boot. It didn't take long until I knew exactly what it was. There was no mistaking that ratty, dyed blonde strand of hair, broken and damaged, with a dark greasy root at the very top.

I didn't need to spring my boot open to know what was inside. She was there. Dead. Just like she had been in that big man's car.

Woozy and far too intoxicated to drive I got back behind the wheel and started the engine. My drive home felt like the personification of autopilot. I don't remember any of my turnings or any hazards I may have observed on the road. All I could think of the entire drive home was that strand of ratty blonde hair. The crumpled-up body I was certain was currently in our boot.

My awareness of my paranoia was subsiding, I was so sleep deprived life felt like a waking nightmare. My earlier plans to come clean and get help were dead in the water, I just wanted this girl to stop following me.

My eyes felt wide and strained as I got out the car. My mind was working at 100 miles a minute and I don't think I'd have been capable of sleep no matter what. I walked around the back of the car to get to my front door and as I passed the boot, the strand of blonde hair was gone. The damage was done, I had bitten off most of the nail on my right index finger throughout this ordeal, blood streamed down my hand.

I stood in the harsh light of the bathroom trying to wash it clean before getting into bed next to my wife. She felt like a stranger by this point. My life had become so consumed by my drinking and this goddamn girl that I had disconnected from my family. My kids were growing up without me present and my wife was raising them alone.

I figured she probably knew about my lies by now, but she still hadn't tried to confront me, so I didn't intend to discuss it with her. No one would employ me in my current state anyway.

I laid in bed, twitching. The girl never once left my mind. Her hollow, sunken sockets for eyes got worse the more I imagined her, and her entire body was almost blanketed by bruises now, like she had been tattooed completely purple.

I looked at the clock at various intervals, desperate to fall asleep and get some relief from this eternal nightmare.

4.55….5.32….6.47….7.09….

9.41

Something was wrong with that last one. It wasn't my bedroom clock. It wasn't the digital display I'd been looking at all night. It was the digital clock on the radio in my car.

The birds sung; the sun blinded me through the windows. It wasn't anything like the sort of thing I was used to driving the graveyard shift. The trees in front of me looked tall, proud, and beautiful. I didn't know how I had made it back to my spot. Even with all my current issues I had never been one to black out like this when drunk. I was truly terrified.

I got out of the car looking at the floor, relieved to get out of the eyeline of the sun, although this did little to calm my nerves. My hands were red with blood from the mangled nails I appeared to have ripped off with my teeth.

As I looked up towards the trees opposite my car, I saw her. Staring back at me, for the very first time with a smile on her face, albeit a sinister one.

I staggered backwards, trying to avoid getting any closer to her. I could feel eyes staring at me. Dog walkers entering and exiting the park, ready to start their morning routine. I was not prepared for the outside world during these active hours. I'm sure my dripping, blood covered hands drew plenty of attention.

I stood, unsteady on my feet staring back at her twisted, smiling face until I heard sirens in the distance. I didn't really register them until they were piercing my eardrums. I couldn't take my eyes off of her.

As the police dragged me to their car, I glimpsed something out of the corner of my eye. Something trapped in the closed boot. This time it wasn't blonde.

I could still see that strand of long auburn hair, silky and wavy, nothing like the ratty blonde strand I had seen before, as the police car drove me away.

I deserved the sentence I got. I killed my wife and our two children, massacred my entire family and still have no recollection. My defence tried to attribute it to sleep deprivation and alcohol induced temporary psychosis. But I knew that was bullshit. I knew it was her.

When I first arrived in prison, I tried to kill myself multiple times. They had me on suicide watch for a while, but my attempts were futile. They'd always find me just in time.

I gave up trying and am prepared to live out my punishment. I don't deserve the release of dying, I should suffer. I still see her every night, staring at me through my cell door, sunken eyes black and terrifying. I wish nightly that my wife would visit me instead, just once.

I was coming around to what the doctors were telling me, that she wasn't real and just a symptom. I was really making steps, but then they moved us around and everyone got new cell mates.

I wasn't happy with mine at first. I was truly terrified. But when I discovered he could see her too I warmed up to him, he was the one that told me writing everything down might be a good thing for me. His dreams had been plagued just like mine.

And after all, he leant me the phone I'm writing on to apologise for getting me fired.

THE PORTAL

I had one hell of a life before all this happened. I took it for granted—don't we all? Now, looking back, I'd give anything to return to that life.

My parents loved me. They were supportive and special and everything a person could ask for. I had a wonderful girlfriend. A fuck ton of friends. Everything a person could really want or need.

It wasn't about money, or being the best at anything really, my life was just about being happy.

Back home, the flowers smelled better, the sun shone brighter, and I don't really remember ever wanting more.

I'm human though. At least I think I am. I get curious. And that damn humming from the closet in my bedroom... It just wouldn't stop. I had to find out what it was.

I tried to ignore it. I sat and tended to the pot plant on my desk and tried to block it out, but I couldn't. It just got louder. I opened it.

It was like suspended liquid metal, swirling between the door frames. I couldn't see my clothes anymore and the sun from my window reflected off it, shooting bright lights into my eyes.

I reached out a hand to touch it, but it just fell straight through. The swirling mass was opaque and I couldn't see my lost limb beyond it. I followed.

What if it was something better? What if there was more on the other side?

One step. Another. A wash of what almost felt like liquid rushed over me, although I stayed dry.

On the other side, there was my room. Just the same as it had been, but somehow… greyer. I don't know what I had expected, but that hadn't been it. The same room with the same window and the same view, yet somehow so unfamiliar.

The sun didn't shine, and the swirling mass of molten portal had gone. The pot plant on my desk had withered and died.

It's been hours and there's no one home. It's only me here. Alone with this laptop. It's the same as the one I had back home except dustier. And the things I've read on it aren't the same.

I took my life for granted. It wasn't filled with war or famine. Murder, abuse and nastiness plagues this place. It's cold here and it's so damn grey.

I don't know how I found this place and I suppose I only have two questions to ask.

How do you all live here… and how can I get home?

Printed in Poland
by Amazon Fulfillment
Poland Sp. z o.o., Wrocław
30 October 2021

57a2d44e-50d0-4016-8448-f3bd1e22a124R01